BORROWED MEMORIES

a novel

MARK FOSS

8TH HOUSE PUBLISHING

8th House Publishing
Montreal, Canada

Cover Design by 8th House Publishing

ISBN
www.8thHousePublishing.com
Set in Garamond, Raleway & Grobold.

LIBRARY AND ARCHIVES CANADA CATALOGUING IN PUBLICATION

Borrowed Memories

SUMMER 2010

WHEN I pull up to the cottage, my father is standing outside the main garage, jamming a steel rod into a metal pipe like he's priming a cannon. It's his latest attempt to build a pole for his air force flag. In phase one, my mother Aida stitched the four edges of the flag onto a steel frame. Once Horace puts the pole together, the frame will swivel freely in the wind, but the flag itself will never sag. It will fly here or at the house in town, wherever he is in residence. Like the Queen of England, he says, without a trace of irony.

He is too preoccupied to notice me hauling my chair across the tailgate, rolling it awkwardly on the grass, and scraping its wheels against the stone patio in front of the guest room on the other side of the garage. Maybe he's forgotten that I'm coming today. More likely he's not wearing his hearing aids. Aida, though, has heard the car. She walks over, eager to help as always. I have to rush back to the car before she tries lifting my suitcase on her own.

"I'll take your briefcase, then," she says.

"It's my computer so don't drop it, please!"

"A computer!"

Her short-term memory may be depleted, but decades of protecting herself against shame have allowed her to pull this mocking voice from a deep recess of her mind. I can't say whether it's conscious. I only know she is aware, on some level, of her mental decline. She will not risk the humiliation of not understanding computers or, perhaps, of failing to remember something previously explained. Her smile is loving, the gentle sarcasm self-directed, magically drawing attention to her ignorance and deflecting it at the same time. Yet her reaction triggers something old in me as well, putting me on the defensive, as if she is trying to take me down a few notches.

AIDA pulls fresh sheets out of the dresser while I unpack the laptop.

"It's just me who's been out here," I tell her. "You don't need to change the bed."

Immediately I regret my remark because it stops her in mid-stride. She grips the sheets tightly against her chest, uncertain what to do next. In her hesitation, I see a way to undo my mistake.

"Do you need some help changing the bed?"

"No, no, I can manage."

Expertly she strips off bedspread, blankets, and sheets. Karen, who converted me to comforters and duvets in the first two weeks of living together, could never get used to this arrangement. It was one more reason she found excuses not to visit the cottage, or if we did, to not stay over.

When Aida flicks the bedspread into place, I catch a whiff of the staleness that never seems to leave the room, no matter how long I air it out. Once the bed is made, she stands uncertain about what to do next.

"Are you hungry?" she asks.

"No, I need to hook up my computer."

"A computer!"

"Maybe Horace needs some help with the flag."

As Aida leaves my room, I sense the knots in my stomach, my tight shoulders, my shortness of breath. I've only been here ten minutes and I'm a wreck. What was I thinking, moving up for a month?

Through the picture window I see Horace and Aida head into the cottage. Even after more than sixty years together, they are inseparable. But with her Alzheimer's and his narcissism, how much longer can he take care of her, especially without a car? Their bungalow in town is nestled into a new subdivision in the north end, far from nowhere. They are living on borrowed time. I guess I'm here to lend them some more.

I set my English-French dictionary on the dresser since the desk is barely big enough for my laptop. I could check most words online now, but I stick with books as a small protest against Google Translate. Soon enough artificial intelligence will replace me altogether so I don't see why I should help it along.

For twenty years, I have worked freelance, translating brochures, annual reports, policy papers, and technical documents, mostly for government. For a while they called me a knowledge worker. Now I'm part of the gig economy. Every time the buzzwords change I get less work. This summer's the slowest in years. So slow I took on a freebie as a favour to a friend. Something for a documentary by a Quebecois filmmaker living in Paris. Maybe, I thought, it might lead to more interesting work or even spark me to create something of my own. But she is late sending me anything. When it comes, I'll be working solely from the words and trying to conjure the images.

Horace emerges from the front door with a fist full of flyers. He marches to the guest room, unaware of how I am watching his move across the grass through the window. Once, his back was as straight as the steel rod he was using to build his flag. Now it leans forward, as if he's up against a headwind.

"You coming?" he asks, as if he's driving. "I want to pick

up a few things."

"So do I."

"You?"

His incredulous face, that look of surprise that I might have needs of my own. I can never get used to it.

❧ 2 ☙

THE "WELCOME TO RIVERTON" sign that boasts a population of 11,000 is wishful thinking. Like other towns along the St. Lawrence River near the Thousand Islands, Riverton struggles to keep people. Unlike Prescott with its fort, and Brockville with its river cruises, Riverton does not have a big draw for tourists. They've talked about building riverfront condos to attract retirees the way Brockville does, but nothing happens. Mostly it's a town of empty storefronts where people shop somewhere else.

Horace's main interest in Riverton is the post office. Every few weeks, he gets another urgent letter from the *Reader's Digest* sweepstakes with breathless requests for urgent action to stay in the running for bonus draws and the grand prize. Sending his response back through a standard mailbox isn't good enough. He goes straight to the source. He's all smiles and chuckles as the postal clerk wishes him luck.

Our business in Riverton finished, we continue down Highway 2 another ten minutes for groceries in Brockville. Horace sits beside me, struggling to read his own writing on the grocery list. He can't remember names of stores but retains his uncanny ability to recall prices down to the last cent.

Throughout my childhood, Horace made me and Aida take separate grocery carts through the cash, creating a semblance of difference to bypass the "limit per family" rules for sale items. If we passed each other in the store, we looked away. I stole glances at Aida all the same, marvelling at the blank look on her face when I bumped into her cart, and said, "Excuse me, Ma'am."

His strategy had the added benefit of keeping us below the "Under 10 items" rule so we all lined up, one after the other, in the Express Lane. I inevitably landed between them, staring at Horace's back while imagining Aida behind me. I would snag a *National Enquirer* and hold it in front of my face, peaking over the top to survey his progress. He would strike up innocuous conversations with the check-out girl to keep her off the scent. Or else he would pretend I had run into his heels with my cart so I could say "I beg your pardon, sir." All part of our elaborate ruse to convince the staff we were strangers. Once we left the store, Horace thought we were scot-free, but I took the game a step further in case the manager was watching. I walked with my plastic bag to the stop sign at the end of the parking lot, slowly, to time my arrival with the car.

"Need a lift?" Horace would ask. He would grin in the rear-view mirror, and I would want to go back to the store and fool them all over again.

AT the Metro, passing through produce en route to bulk food, Horace tears off a few green grapes, pops them in his mouth, and spits the seeds on the floor. He grabs a handful of Voortman cookies and slides them into the plastic bag I hold open for him. I keep my eyes on the "No Sampling" sign so I can avoid seeing him take a cookie for the road.

"They've got the roast chicken you like," I tell him.
"Not here. The girl knows me at the other place."
He looks at the price of ice cream.
"They're out of their minds," he says.

AT Giant Tiger, he holds on tightly to the cart, weaving his way through the clothes, teen idol posters, and farting gnomes, toward the food. I point out there's a reason the food is cheaper here: the milk in his cart will turn sour in a few days.

"It'll be fine," he says.

AT Food Basics, he emerges with his cheap bread, cereal, and other staples too irresistible to pass up. The vegetable soup cans in his basement are corroded black, as if someone has popped them in the microwave. He can always use a few more.

THE clerk at Value-Mart marks down the price of his roast chicken, although the sale doesn't start until the next day. The ice cream prices are better there, too. In the frozen food section, I help pile twenty-four boxes of Stouffer's meals into the cart. At the cash, he hands the young cashier a box of frozen chicken breasts.

"Cutting," he says.

I expect a puzzled look, but Tammi—from her nametag—is well-versed in the ways of seniors. She understands immediately that Horace wants her to cut out the two-for-one coupons from the Stouffer's boxes. Her pierced lip lowers a little in contempt, but she says nothing. The coupons may not be intended for same-day purchase, but what does she care if he gets a discount from food he hasn't bought yet? Yet she still makes her displeasure clear by hacking them out slowly, and only for twelve of the boxes. When the chicken breasts fall onto the conveyor belt out of the gaping holes, I manoeuvre them back inside the boxes. They probably fall out again when Horace throws them in the bags.

"I guess that's it," he says.

"I need to make a stop."

"I've got everything we need."

"Something for my work."

"You?"

At Staples, I buy three telephone extension cables so I can string a line from the jack in the cottage to the guest room. It's a half-assed solution, one that will only give me access to dial-up.

"I'm done," I tell him. "You want a cold drink?"

"Take a drive by the school, would you?"

Horace grew up in Brockville but bought the bungalow in Riverton because it was five minutes' closer to the cottage. The school is not exactly on the way home, but I know better than to question his logic or to remind him about the frozen chicken in the back.

I slow to a crawl, pacing our progress against the time it will take to relive his childhood memories. He is silent, though, which makes me anxious. Maybe he has come here not to relive his memories but rather to find them.

"Isn't this where you buried the pennies?" I ask.

"That's right."

"How did you get the dollar out of the grate again?"

"Oh."

"Didn't you get some fishing line and chewing gum, or something?"

"That's right. Me and Bob. We used a sinker to give it some weight."

I'm tempted to recite the rest for him, the way I wrote

about it in his memoirs. How Horace and Bob retrieved the silver dollar, with its single likeness of George V, trading it for one hundred smaller versions of the king at the candy store. How Horace buried his share on the grounds of Prince of Wales Public School where they sang "God Save the King" every morning. How he dug up his royal treasure every so often, removing a single coin from the stash, cleaning the sovereign's face, and heading back to the store for more penny candy. How he sucked on the jawbreakers to make them last as long as possible.

"Bob spent all his pennies that same afternoon at the candy store," he says. "He was impulsive. I said to him, 'Bob, what's your hurry? Conscription will get you.' I should have made him hold on to those pennies. You take care of your pennies, and the dollars look after themselves. Spinning right out of control. Thank God I had Bob on my shoulder."

It frightens me, sometimes, how I can follow the workings of his mind. How he jumps from the pennies to Bob's enlistment and death to his own fateful spin just before the war ended. Falling out of the sky from ten thousand feet in his Harvard aircraft with a student pilot, Horace could see the trees. Somehow the plane righted itself in time. For years, it was chance. Then, after a book I gave him on the Harvard, he understood it was a design flaw. Finally, it became divine intervention. The Creator had saved him—a deity, unrecognizable from scripture, charged solely with the preservation of Horace Pyefinch, and apparently channelled through the spirit of his friend Bob.

Karen thought if I spent half as much time trying to understand her as I did Horace our marriage might have lasted longer. But the truth is worse: understanding Horace is no work at all for me. What's harder is sublimating my own history, knowing that he only cares about his own memories.

He is silent the rest of the way back, although he points to the turnoff to our cottage road as if I've never been here before. At the bottom of the hill, I glance at the notice for the annual meeting of cottagers taped to the "Private Road" sign. On Sunday, we will once again discuss paving the gravel. Last year, like every year it comes up, Horace argued it was a waste of money, and the summer residents sided with him. Since then, two more cottages have been turned into winter homes. The balance of power is shifting to the permanent residents, and they probably smell blood.

I haven't told anyone that Horace has signed over the cottage to me, nor have I reminded Horace. He only did it for estate planning, not to lose his vote. But word has got round that I'm the official voice for our family. I faxed my proxy vote for the status quo so I could avoid the meeting. I can't bear the spectacle of Horace unable to marshal the old guard one last time or not understanding why his own vote no longer counted.

As we approach the monstrous home of our treasurer, who will be hosting the meeting this year, Horace follows my own finger, out of boredom rather than real interest.

"I lost some silver dollars over there once," I tell him. "You helped me get them back."

He stares at the house blankly.

With great ceremony, I had wrapped the silver dollars in scrap cloth before placing them inside the velvet Crown Royal bag. The package was just small enough to be stuffed inside the hole of the tree that sat on an abandoned property down the road from our cottage. I imagined returning one day, grey and wizened after a lifetime of wandering, to retrieve this stash. Oh, how it would evoke bittersweet memories of my life as a child. I rubbed my fingers one last time along the raised surface of the silver dollars, tracing the imprint of a voyageur and his First Nations guide paddling their birchbark canoe.

I stuck my hand inside the hole to feel for a ledge or something to snag the velvet on its descent. There was only empty space. I released the bag anyway, praying it would stop within reach. But there was no divine intervention. The birchbark canoes spun end-over-end inside the hollow, throwing voyageurs and their guides violently from their seats. Clutching in vain at the slippery gunwales, they tumbled in freefall, arms and legs flailing. The old tales were true: they had fallen off the ends of the Earth. Helpless to combat what fate had in store, they did not know which was worse: the certain death of a landing or a journey without end.

I didn't tell Horace the whole story, just enough to get advice from him—the coin-retrieval expert. No gum this time, but rather a hook, line, and sinker to fish out the bag. The whole business from start to finish took about a half hour, not long enough for wrinkled lines of wisdom to form on my face. At the end of summer, the property was sold, and the tree chopped down. I would have to outwit time some other way.

 3

IN LATE afternoon, I string the three telephone cords together across the lawn from the cottage, and cover the connections with tape to mask them from overnight dampness. For reasons unknown, Horace pulled the phone jack out of the wall in the guest room last year. He can't remember doing it, let alone how to re-connect the yellow and black wires. I could find his old tester set, the one we used to hook into the neighbour's line in the 1970s before ours was re-connected in July. Maybe that would help, or maybe he would only remember how much he'd forgotten.

Horace began installing telephones for Bell Canada in the month that Princess Elizabeth registered for war service. He took up the job again after completing his own service in the air force as a pilot instructor in Scotland. By then technology had changed, and he uninstalled hundreds of crank sets. Bell junked them, unable to imagine their future value as antiques, but Horace kept a few. Years later, he used the old phones to connect the cottage and the waterfront. We need an intercom, he'd said, in case of a nuclear attack. By then he was managing telephone contracts for the distant early warning system—the DEW Line. If the Soviets pushed the red button to send armed missiles over the Arctic, his boss needed to reach him instantly. If he was working on the dock, Aida was supposed to relay the message through the intercom. Each time it rang, I was relieved Aida was calling us up for lunch and not announcing World War III.

"WHAT'S all this about?" Horace asks.

"It's a dew line."

No wince, no grin, no guffaw, no inkling he remembers his role in protecting Canada's North during the Cold War.

"I'm covering it up to protect it against the dew," I tell him.

"The do what?"

"The moisture."

"You ought to put a phone in Ivan's bedroom," says Aida. She has appeared out of nowhere, still eager to defend my interests.

"What does he need that for?"

She stands quietly, unable to retain the question in her mind, and then moves to carry the grocery bags into the cottage. Aida speaks on instinct now, incapable of stringing two thoughts together. A flash of resignation from Horace. He misses their small battles, even if they irritate him. Or else he's pushing away thoughts of his own failing memory, all those years climbing telephone polls, installing and tearing out wire. As for me, I can barely remember what I translated last week or why it seemed so important.

For all my weekend visits this summer, I've been tapping into the neighbour's Wi-Fi, but now it's password protected. I could go to the public library in Riverton or drive a little farther to the Home Depot or Starbucks in Brockville. Maybe I will offer to share the connection costs with the neighbour. Anything but try to explain Wi-Fi again to Horace when we still make do with a rotary phone.

For the past few years, I've been transferring all his voicemails to a digital recorder. I suppose I think they will have value for me one day as antiques. For the next month, I will be privy to every thought, desire, and whim that he cares to express in real time without the filter of technology. Now who's trapped?

 4

HOLDING my breath, I try connecting to my email through the system I've rigged up. In years past, either Horace or Aida would inevitably pick up the telephone in the cottage and break the link to the modem. Now I can add the fear that one of them will stumble on the line spread across the lawn, breaking a hip along with my connection. The modem whines as it accelerates, a sound I had forgotten I knew. The first email from the filmmaker has arrived from Paris. I feel like Marconi on Signal Hill, receiving the letter "s" in the first transatlantic wireless transmission. But I doubt that Marconi spelled his name in lower-case letters.

> Tentative
> 8/4/2010 4:34 PM
> From: mia hakim
> To: Ivan Pyefinch
>
> Dear Ivan,
> I don't like to explain too much. Maybe translate the first few pages and send them to me? Then I can see if this tentative is a good idea. I appreciate your generosity.
> mia

By "tentative", she means "attempt", but I hear the English sense of the word as well: she is hesitant. I am, too. When I look at what she has sent, I feel like I've jumped inside the middle of her world without a map. I translate quickly, as if that will help me understand.

Busy people, half-broken down scooters, children with arms full of bread. Little fruit trucks carrying hopes and dreams. Housewives emerging out of low-rise buildings. Puddles on a road full of potholes. Night falls on Sfax as Karim and I walk through the roads, trying to find ourselves again. We have not seen each other for many years, not since he lived in Montreal. To others, we were unlikely companions. For us, our differences as Muslim and

Jew were less important than our connection to Tunisia.

Karim tells me: "Every night at the house, my father read the Quran aloud in front of the family. But he was the only one to pray. Ramadan was, above all, about the warmth of family dinners. I don't buy into everything in the Islam of today. I don't like the infiltration of religion into politics. During Eid, the holiday of Sacrifice, the Imam's prayer ended with insults against secular Muslims, communists, Christians, and Jews. I wanted to leave. Religion for me is a direct relationship with God. I like prayers at dawn because there are so few people."

Side by side, two open books, ancient editions of the Quran and the Torah. Images of prayers at dawn filmed in a mosque and in a synagogue.

I tell him that religious Jews also pray at dawn. But women, because they give birth and are closer to divine creation, are exempted. Karim explains the Arab word for Jew— "Yehoud"— literally means, "he who has followed the path toward the One God". He tells me that to understand a language you have to break words down to their roots.

DURING my childhood, Horace and Aida offered no prayers except a few words of grace at Thanksgiving and Christmas. But I said them on my own at bedtime. I was determined to help ward off the prowlers that Horace so feared would show up during our weekends away at the cottage. With both hands folded to my chin, the way I had seen on television, I cited a thesaurus of property crimes to ensure our house was not burgled, broken-into, or robbed. Was it "A-men" or "Ah-men"? I hedged my bets, saying it both ways. Unlike Karim, I never thought to break down the word to its roots. Part of me wants to tell Mia this story, but I simply send off her translation. Our tentative is not about sharing my stories with her.

AFTER setting the table, husking the corn, and boiling the water, Aida looks expectantly at Horace. Meal planning once filled up so much of her mind, and nothing has come in to replace it. So she stands, a fixed smile, a little vacant, a little un-certain. Inexplicably, she is in the way—here, in her own realm, in the kitchen she has inhabited every summer since 1951, in the space she insisted they renovate when building the new addition. Is that what's bothering her? That cupboards cover the space where the back door once stood, that she no longer has to stop washing dishes to let Horace into the refrigerator? The fridge, newly purchased for the renovation thirty years ago, now needs a kick at the bottom for the seal to hold. Even Horace has forgotten this trick, and I can almost feel the cold escaping from the gap. He moves about, oblivious to anyone or anything other than the task at hand. Ignoring the Stouffer's boxes already opened at the store, he tears open three new ones for tonight's dinner. He has the good grace to choose the same frozen meat loaf for everyone, even if he can only fit two plastic containers at a time in the microwave. Through the splattered door, they bump into each other on the turnstile until they simply don't move and the plate underneath keeps spinning.

"Four minutes," Horace says.

His words are directed at me, the official timekeeper for corn-on-the-cob. He used to set the clock seven minutes ahead so he wouldn't be late for work, but now gravity has pulled its two hands permanently to six-thirty. If only stopping time were really so easy.

"I think we should test Aida behind the wheel," he says. "She's still got her licence."

"I can drive," Aida says. She sounds bemused, as if she's bringing us all up to speed on what is obvious to her.

"We can take the back roads," Horace says. "I'll sit beside her. There's no one out there to bother us. Why the hell not?"

"Your test is coming up in a week or two," I tell him. "I'm sure it will go well, and then you won't need to bother."

"Well, it's a backup plan."

"Plan B."

"That's right."

"Corn's ready," I tell him. "Did you want to get it?"

Deflect, redirect, put off, all those strategies to avoid conflict that drove Karen nuts. The tactic works with Horace, pushing away any thought of failure from his mind. It seems to work on me as well. Here I am, unwilling to speculate on how they will manage if he doesn't get his licence back. How much of my life is it reasonable to give up for them, and for how long?

As Horace and Aida get settled at the table, I zap their meals for a few more seconds, hoping the extra dose of radiation doesn't kill what little goodness is left. My own meal is still hot to the touch.

Horace devours his corn like he's got somewhere to go, wipes off his buttery fingers, and digs into the meatloaf. Aida is more methodical, spreading butter on the corn with a knife instead of rolling it in the groove left by Horace, as if she has all the time in the world. Her meatloaf is getting cold, but unlike Horace, she won't complain. She will accept the temperature of her meal, grateful to be served for once, having forgotten, perhaps, what is considered optimal.

"I guess Karen was too busy to come," Aida says.

Horace doesn't remind Aida that Karen and I broke up two years ago. *Broke up* sounds like an explosive force that shattered us into immeasurable shards. Ours was simply a relationship stretched too thin until the gaping holes took over. The petty quarrels and resentments ate away at us until we got tired of defending our positions.

It probably doesn't help Aida's confusion that I still wear my wedding ring. Nostalgia, false hope, or inertia? Maybe all three at once.

"Look, Ivan's got a tattoo on his wrist," Aida says.

"Jesus, he's had that for years."

I wait for more, an outburst directed my way. His irritation with Aida's fading memory seems to have surpassed his rage at me. Or has he forgotten?

In 1986, I was twenty-three years old and newly graduated from university when I had the image of a silver dollar imprinted on the underside of my right wrist. I had told Karen the tattoo was a whim as she was always on my case to be more spontaneous. She saw through me, knowing I would have planned it all out. Yes, it was a declaration of independence. I knew the desecration of my body would outrage Horace. Further, I chose the image of a coin as a rebuke against his obsessiveness with money. And there was more to it than that. With the government introducing a new dollar coin, I had wanted to preserve the classic image of the voyageur and First Nations man in the canoe. Even as I was starting the next phase of my life, I was dragging my feet, desperately needing to keep myself fixed in time. I didn't need to retrieve a silver dollar from the boughs of a tree anymore to evoke nostalgia. Instead, I would embody it.

On my first visit back home with the tattoo, I had grown tired of Horace waiting to notice.

"What do you think?" I had demanded, thrusting out my arm.

He didn't understand at first, probably thinking it was just dirt.

"You've got to be kidding," he'd said, finally. "Aida, did you see this? Our son."

He had rolled his steaming corn on the square of butter over and over until it formed a deep hollow. Then he turned the cob over and over on his plate, salting the same sides two or three times. After a few bites, he had left it uneaten, and picked at his steak and mashed potatoes. He got up from the table and walked to the garage. Maybe it was an invitation at reconciliation: I could offer to help him with whatever project he had on the go, like I had always done. Instead, I returned home to my life in Ottawa without saying goodbye. I had hurt him and I was free.

He wrote me a letter and I could smell the mixture of butter and sawdust on the page. He agonized that a tattoo would jeopardize me getting a good job in government. He said I had destroyed his dreams. If only I had asked for his advice, he said, he would have steered me on the right path. He confessed he had been crying, experiencing a loss so great he could only equate it to the death of his best friend Bob Wright in the war.

He had spoken of Bob once or twice before. Did the two figures in the canoe on my wrist remind him of childhood adventures with his friend? Did my rejection of his values trigger some unresolved grief about his loss? Or was the tattoo incidental, one of any number of possible entry points to pry open the past?

All these questions came later. When I read his letter, I simply resented how Bob had overshadowed my act of independence. I shoved it in a drawer, never imagining how the resurrected friend would take over all of our lives.

5

KAREN AND I French-kissed for the first time playing Spin the Bottle at a birthday party when we were nine years old. Our mouths were open when we got close. Maybe we were trying to speak at the same time, to voice our embarrassment. A slip of the tongue, then, nothing more. Yet didn't we both regularly haul out this shared memory, charging it with meaning to suit our personal agendas. In the early years, so full of ourselves, we would show off our special connection in front of friends. Alone together, I would tease Karen that our marriage was based on the fibres of the shag carpet that stopped the bottle before it reached Heather or Fran. Later, Karen would evoke the incident as an early example of how I silenced her self-expression.

A few days after the fateful birthday party, probably by Tuesday recess, I was back to playing foot hockey with my friends, and Karen did whatever she did. Only in early adolescence did the incident resurface, unspoken between us but clearly present. In high school, where we both took music, we averted our gaze by mutual consent. Easily done since I sat behind and to her left in the brass section. By eleventh grade, when I dropped out of music to play hockey for the school team, she was First Alto Sax in the concert and stage bands.

At school assemblies, I would watch her stand for jazz solos, envious at her self-assurance, a little forlorn that we travelled in different orbits. Everyone thought she would pursue music. Instead, she took the same translation degree as I did at the University of Ottawa. In a room full of strangers, our eyes locked in recognition, and we gravitated toward each other by default.

Our ambivalence made a kind of sense because we were studying translation out of fear rather than love. Both of our fathers, Horace and Derrick, were air force veterans who coasted into the post-war era with twelfth grade education, working for the same companies their entire careers before retiring with good pensions. White, middle-class anglos, they both voted Progressive Conservative, reacted with suspicion to multiculturalism in general, and resented special status for Quebec in particular. They were determined that we, their children, would be bilingual to get those good government jobs. On the heels of the Quiet Revolution, when I was in fourth grade, Horace signed me up for extra French lessons on Saturday mornings to prepare me for the Loud Revolution to come. By university, I had no other talents apart from the language arts so I fell into translation almost naturally. But Karen gave up music for a more practical career to satisfy her father, and blamed everyone but herself for the choice.

At forty-eight, childless, bored with dissecting French words at the Translation Bureau and interpreting my long periods of silence, Karen picked up the sax again. She started busking, for fun, on weekends, and pressed me to rent a trombone. My lips tingled from the mouthpiece. They were flabby from disuse like the rest of my body. I gave it up, joining a beer hockey league to relive my own past glories and get into shape. Then some hotshot brass players asked her to join them for a gig. Soon she was out three nights a week to practice, and playing on weekends. All this around the same time that Horace and Aida needed more help. I gave up hockey and spent weekends in Riverton. Our separate lives provoked resentment for both of us, but not the urgency to do anything about it. Of course she left me for the trombonist, a young francophone with tight abs and a three octave range. The kind of guy whose tongue never slipped.

I've had a few dates through the online sites. Before I landed Horace's station wagon, I was looking for someone within walking distance of my condo. Now that I'm here at the cottage, I've adjusted my profile again. Interests: "Caregiving for my elderly parents who are declining mentally". I don't believe in these sites, especially the ones that promise to match you based on interests and sensibility. Where is the magic in algorithms? I want the hands of fate, guided by carpet fibres if necessary, to point out my next love.

THE reflection from my table lamp makes it impossible to see anything through the patio window, but I feel the vibration of a passing ship in the channel. I should really have stayed in the cottage to be sociable and to keep an ear and an eye on Horace and Aida. Yet here I am, on the other side of the DEW line, trusting that any emergency will happen in broad daylight.

Response
8/4/2010 8:34 PM
From: mia hakim
To: Ivan Pyefinch

Dear Ivan,
I like what you have done, although it is strange to see my words

take on a new life in English. It's as if I see them for the first time all over again. It makes me nervous that the woman in these scenes seems like someone else. But I knew this would happen and it's what I wanted — to give myself some distance. It's almost as if you are writing the story, and I get to discover it. I have sent you some more text. It is late in Paris so I wish you good night. Merci.

mia

At a red light, Karim produces his surprise: a copy of a telephone directory from 1937. I find the surname and discover the real first name of my grandfather, Papa Chichi. On the Avenue de Paris we ask around, and an old Arab remembers my family. Am I here to take back the building? I shake my head, embarrassed. I do not want to be one of those Tunisian Jews who come back for reparation or to bask in the warmth of nostalgia on the beaches. I only want to understand.

I think I recognize my grandfather's building, the long ramp of staircases with leather banisters and marble steps ending with a sort of toboggan jump, where, as a child, I slid down to jump off the stairs. Leaving the building, Karim points out the grand synagogue of Tunis, freshly painted, standing solemnly under the sun, well guarded by armed police. I have no reaction. Karim seems affronted that my grandfather lived opposite the synagogue and I don't remember. But I never set foot in this synagogue, or any other. Maybe this is not his house, after all.

I COULD never mistake my grandfather's house in Brockville. Out with Horace, if we are not driving by the school, we make a point to pass by his childhood home. He will tell me stories about tobogganing down the hill or playing hockey in the creek with Bob, how he switched from the Catholic Church to the Baptists so he could be with his friend for Sunday service. As we drive up the hill, he will name the streets where he delivered newspapers, always first to hang his empty bag around the lamppost. He once wrote a letter to the editor where he thanked the newspaper for teaching him good values.

Before this crisis with his driver's licence, when Horace and Aida were more independent and my visits less frequent, I would sometimes drive by the old house on my own. I've never been inside, and had a fantasy it would be for sale one day. I didn't want to buy it, but rather simply to walk through the rooms, and imagine the lives unfolding during the Depression. How at the dinner table an older brother once threw a knife at Horace that stuck into the wall behind him. How Horace's younger brother resented Bob getting all his attention. On this tour, the presence of Horace himself would be a distraction. From his stories I have formed my own impressions of his past, and prefer to relive them silently.

Karim resents playing interpreter.

He provokes me, saying, "You should speak Arabic. You're Tunisian."

"And how could I have not forgotten the language, leaving here as a child?"

"You quit Arab school before leaving your father's house. And then you took the trouble to learn Hebrew in Israel."

Silence. Not a breath of Arabic, Hebrew, or French in the air.

"When I was young, I liked French because it opened a window on the world," Karim says, finally. "At nineteen I left for Damascus to improve my skills in Arabic by studying law, but I still wrote letters to my father in French. He would not answer. I was furious, but he said, write to me in Arabic and I will respond. That was how I came to bring my Arabic books to Montreal with me. My father was right.

"In Montreal, I couldn't find work, even with my Master's degree, except in a call centre. I gave courses in Arabic to students, journalists, poets, and women. As a joke, I would tell them the course would serve no purpose here, but at least they could converse in paradise. And then I'd had enough, and came home."

IT'S close to midnight when I finish the translation. I should let the words ferment overnight, but I feel an intense need to share them right away, as if they are truly mine. Or maybe I want to prove to Mia that I can capture experiences so foreign to my own. After sending her the email, I shut down the computer and crawl into bed.

What would Horace make of Karim's story? Would he identify with the proud father? Would he fume at the immigrant who did not appreciate what Canada had to offer? Most likely, he would puzzle over the idea that someone fluent in French could not find good work in Quebec. For Horace, language is the only card that matters in Canada. That Quebec might discriminate against a French-speaking person because of an accent, skin colour, or a name that was difficult to pronounce has never entered his lexicon. Sheltered in Riverton, at the cottage, or in a gated community in Florida that managed to keep out Black people, he has had little exposure to multiculturalism, except on the news. He might get riled up about immigrants swelling the ranks of the unemployed, but the real fight of his life has been official bilingualism, beginning with his own father.

On visits to my grandparents in their Ottawa apartment in the 1970s, Horace tried to convince his father that Trudeau's policies were a threat to unilingual anglophones. My grandfather, still resentful about Conservative policies during the Depression, supported Trudeau's vision of a Just Society where reason triumphed over passion. I lay on the shag carpet, half listening to their arguments and half straining to hear the animals fight on *Untamed World.* The sound from the TV was coming from behind me, out of the earphone draped over my grandfather's standing ashtray. He used the earphone to avoid conflict with the sound from my grandmother's black and white portable TV in the kitchen.

The strikes and parries, the entrenched positions, and fresh stalemates came at me from all directions, both connected and divorced from the images on the screen. Karen once asked me when I shut down my emotions as a child. I think it was lying in the shag rug to avoid the smoky blows, recording dialogue in my head, that I chose reason over passion.

Our own television, a black and white Electrohome, stood on the floor beside the cupboard with the louvred doors that held the old set. Constant switching of channels during commercials made the picture start slipping into snow, with the French CBC invading the English channels. Horace filed the butt end of a broken hockey stick to fit over the channel selector. One poke check would bring everything back to normal.

He bought a small black and white Panasonic, which sat atop the Electrohome except on weekends when I took it into my room for the hockey game. Once, after Ken Dryden posted another shut-out for the Montreal Canadiens, I stumbled onto naked women on the Panasonic. I stayed up late, switching from reason to passion.

I would study descriptions of French movies in the television guide for signs of erotica as if they were lessons in *Ici on parle français,* my high school textbook. The films didn't help my French since I kept the sound down. I waited for the French women to invade my silent screen, and I could hear Horace watching the late news on the new colour Sony, cursing the election of René Levesque and the renewed threat of separatism in Quebec. He stomped off to bed, and my ear stayed tuned, rabbit-like, for Aida's discreet tread on the stairs. My bedroom had wood panelling and two louvred doors whose slats aimed down. I was convinced she could see light or perhaps even sense heat emanating from the French films and would pull open the doors.

I rolled the UHF band into no-man's land, turned down the contrast, threw a towel over the cathode ray tubes glimmering at the back of the set, and feigned sleep. From the blur of static as I retuned the UHF channel, naked women emerged at my command. They didn't speak of love, only mouthed the words. It was enough, my own quiet revolution.

 6

I AM DREAMING of being lost in Tunis when the sound of hammering on the other side of the wall jars me awake. I resist the childhood urge to rush out of bed and offer Horace my help. So many times I stood at his side, bored and resentful, with no role to play except to witness his mind at work. All those ingenious solutions to problems that held no interest to me. I wish he would give up on this flag idea and spend more time reading the driver's manual. He has supreme confidence or else he is pushing away his fear.

Mia has sent another file overnight. I translate it right away, hoping her story will drown out the noise in the garage and in my head.

Karim knows my primal attachment to Tunisia is connected to my lost childhood. But he resents how the Jews left, as if his sense of cultural abandonment is more important than those who lost everything. It's the oldest conflict between us, the one we've inherited.

With a kind of vulgar arrogance, I throw back the complaint most often voiced: "The Arabs threw us out at Independence." Never mind my own little story never touched this path of history.

"The responsibility is shared," Karim retorts. "The Jews left the Arabs to be closer culturally to the French colonialists. They chose to speak French and send their children to French high schools, and not Arab ones."

Silence.

"I swear, Karim, that this time even if I have to cry out this entire sea, I will not give up until we understand each other."

"Thank God," he says.

"I've done my homework. I read a book on the history of Jews in Tunisia, and I studied the links you sent me."

"Should I applaud?"

I'M starting to like Karim. He doesn't put up with any bullshit. He's got an attitude, although I can't imagine how any of this would work in a film.

By the time I'm dressed, Mia has already responded to my translation. She doesn't like "Should I applaud?", preferring something closer to the French, like "Do you want me to build you a statue?" Another writer who can't resist back-seat driving. Except this time I have doubts. The subject is so utterly foreign to me. Maybe I should use expressions that suggest this strangeness or, at least, try a little harder.

When Karen and I broke our frequent silences, we tried to speak the language we had learned from self-help books and spiritual development weekends. I could never bring myself to talk of the "pain body" without scare quotes. But for all that, we were white middle-class Canadians who grew up in the same city around the same time with the same ambivalent relationship to religion. Eventually, one of us would raise a white flag. No reconciliation. More an unspoken decision to pretend the conflict never happened. Karim and Mia, I think, have a better way. They never sink into silence so long that the sores fester. Someone interjects, not with platitudes, but with sarcasm. Or even raw truth. I can feel the tension between them, this desperate desire to break through their differences.

Through the patio window I see Horace walk toward the cliff with his air force flag on its new pole. I'm sure he's already thinking about Remembrance Day. He starts trying on the uniform in October to make sure it still fits, and gets Aida to adjust the medals. He never paid attention to any of this while I was growing up. He wrote away for his medals in 1995, and they arrived in time for his first parade. He marched to celebrate the golden anniversary of victory in Europe and the defeat of the separatists in the Quebec referendum two weeks before. The Creator was looking out for Canada, he told me.

My Blackberry pings with another message from Mia.

"Maybe 'Thank God' should be 'Praise Be to God,'" she writes. "Or maybe we should leave it as "'*Hamdullah*'."

I write back: "Maybe instead of 'God,' we could say 'the Creator'? And instead of 'Should I applaud?' or 'Do you want me to put you up a statue?', what about 'Do you want a medal?'"

 7

HORACE PUT together our first dock by pouring cement down a wooden chute he had erected over the fifty-foot cliff. The cement landed in a bed of rocks tapered toward the water's edge. He had etched the date in the wet cement, cured it for a week to keep it strong (like his own father had taught him), and then removed the wooden frame. The second dock, set up parallel to the boat rack, was made of wood and connected to pipes he picked up cheap at the auto wreckers on the third concession. As for the giant wheel that hauled up the boat, he bargained the fellow down to save fifty bucks.

I remember all these stories clearly, although they happened before I was born. Other stories I push aside, like the time he was heading home to Ottawa for the week, and asked me to cure the cement for the blocks he had built to hold our house trailer. I proudly watered the two blocks on the west side just like he had showed me, never thinking I should do the ones on the east as well. He was more disappointed than angry at having a son with so little talent for anything practical. For years, in sleepovers with friends, I half expected the trailer to collapse under the weight of its imperfect foundation.

I can never push any story away entirely, as much as I would like to. As the self-anointed custodian of cottage history, I carry layers of memory that open unbidden with a glance at a boulder, a door, a tree, a spray can. Our family's time here is outside history, full of meaning only to ourselves, and increasingly, to me alone. I prepare for a time when Horace and Aida will not remember anything, and I bounce from a compulsion to preserve the cottage on their behalf to a desire to let someone else create a new family history here. I'm not certain whether keeping the cottage or letting it go would sow more loss.

Horace designed self-winding mechanisms for both the boat rack and our second dock. In autumn, we crank them high enough to keep the front feet away from the grip of the ice. In summer, we let them down gently. A few years back, after a big spring storm, someone's pontoon floated down river and lodged into the rocks on the west side of the dock. Using this as a base, he built a third dock. In the fall, he puts a tepee-shaped wooden structure on this new dock to ward off snow. He suspends the whole shebang above the water with high-strength steel attached to the fence along the cliff. This year he has had problems with the dock, which he is determined to solve.

None of us swim anymore. The motorboat, which hasn't been in the water for forty years, sits on a trailer whose wheels have sunken three inches into the ground. I no longer sail my Laser. With the well they put in a few years ago, Horace doesn't even need to climb down the steps to the waterfront. Yet with his flag flying proud and free, he is full of ambition to repair the third dock. Maybe he'll get the wooden canoe in the water again. It would sit perfectly on the dock. This canoe, which Horace once used for fishing trips with Bob in the 1930s, has been sitting across two wooden horses inside the back garage for at least twenty-five years.

"That canoe is heavy, isn't it?" I say.

"Not in the water," Horace says.

He laughs at his own joke, and who am I to spoil his jovial mood?

The two of us eat breakfast alone while Aida sips her tea in front of the oversized patio door. Her pills to fight Alzheimer's remain untouched in the egg cup sitting beside her cereal on the table. Horace is too enthused about his new project to harangue Aida about not taking her medication.

"Did you see the flag?" he asks.

"Lookin' good," I tell him.

"Aid did a great job at sewing it up tight."

Aid—it's been ages since I've heard Horace use this pet name. He pronounces it "I'd," but I often hear it as "aid," as in "help." The indispensable assistant and trusty sidekick, who, unlike me, enjoys standing at Horace's side. But today, since Mia's French scenario refers to Eid al-Adha as Aïd, I also hear "sacrifice."

What Aida hears I don't know. She keeps sipping her tea, oblivious. No doubt she's forgotten her role in the flag project. Maybe the sign of affection from Horace has been so long in coming she no longer recognizes it. I have been dreading the day that she no longer remembers me or cannot say my name. It hasn't occurred to me, until now, that she may forget her own as well.

I bring round her cereal.

"I've poured the milk," I tell her. "It's going to get all soggy if you don't eat."

"Well, now, we wouldn't want that to happen!"

I wait patiently until she puts the bowl down after four bites, and then offer the pills and water. I can't push too much because she resists attempts to control her. A sudden streak of independence at eighty-three has come at the wrong time for the wrong reasons.

She once took pills without protest, popping hormone supplements for mood swings on the advice of her doctor. Maybe this is what levelled off her emotions during my adolescence, although even as a child I remember her as a ghostly presence. Flat and still, except when angling for Horace's attention. Although my skin was not so bad, she also put me on antibiotics for acne. She believed our pills were tiny skipping stones to help ride the surface of menopause and adolescence without ever feeling their depth. Now her still waters are increasingly marked by emotional turbulence. Meanwhile, the scar tissue underneath the skin of my shoulders makes my acupuncturist's needles spring up like unruly geysers.

"All these?" she says.

"They're good for what ails you."

She laughs, accepting my words at face value, just as I take it on faith that her memory loss would be worse without the medication. In other words, I'm still skipping stones. This time round, however, there will be no reckoning thirty years down the line.

Standing behind her chair, I notice how thin her hair has become, probably hastened by decades of scrubbing chemicals into her roots. Now, without weekly trips to the salon or her own treatments in the bathroom, her hair has turned unapologetically grey. Years ago—before suntan lotion became sunscreen—she also squeezed oily liquid out of the tube of *Bain de Soleil* onto her face. She pronounced it

"Bane," which was more accurate since the sun dried her skin prematurely, leaving deeply imbedded streams and tributaries bereft of moisture. She knew the effects of the facelift wouldn't last forever. Sure enough, twenty years later, the wrinkles are back with a vengeance. Another dam that's cracking.

I remove the blue tarp covering the cushions on the glass table, and set up the chaise lounge on the patio for Aida. The fabric she used to recover the cushions in the mid-1970s is wearing thin. Through the holes, my fingers brush up against the original pink vinyl, which is coarse and brittle to the touch.

"Horace and I are going down to the dock to work for a while," I tell her.

"Do you want some help?"

"I think we'll be fine. I'll let you know."

"I'll be right here," she says, and I want to believe her.

8

Medals
8/6/2010 10:25 PM
From: mia hakim
To: Ivan Pyefinch

Dear Ivan,
I don't know this expression "Do you want a medal?" but it sounds right. It has the sarcastic tone that I imagine coming out of Karim. He pushes me to understand more of my own history and then makes fun of me when I try. I also like the idea of earning a medal for knowledge instead of for killing people or swimming fast in a pool. Yes, I want a medal for learning, but it will never happen because there is no finish line. I've sent you some more text. Have you any experience of exile? I am just wondering. It's not a job interview. I know you're doing this for free.
mia

I come from an Arab country, but I've lived in Canada for thirty years. I have never returned to the country of my childhood. I was too afraid. No one could guarantee that juxtaposing my images of the past with the present would not cover my memories with a layer of reality too real, or worse, erase them altogether. I could not risk losing my few memories. It was enough to cope with the adoption of a new identity, which was already complex.

Karim asks what I remember, and I am eager to show off.

There was the broken dam, the cafés near the port that smelled of the sea, my grandfather's stall in the souk where he sold fabric, the market for camels, the earthen house where I spent starry nights in the desert, the garden with thirteen fruit trees, the silkworm factory, the jasmine veils behind blue-studded doors....

Stop, he says. These are postcards from a country that no longer exists.

Re: Medals
8/7/2010 6:31 PM
From: Ivan Pyefinch
To: mia hakim

I know nothing of exile, but I do know about coming and going. In my childhood home, we had an apple tree in our backyard. Just one, not thirteen. My father pampered that tree for years so it would bear fruit. Finally, after nearly twenty years it produced beautiful apples. But by that time my father was retiring, and they were moving to the country. He offered to come back each year to spray the tree for the new owner. Of course, the new owner politely declined. Later, through a neighbour, I discovered the new owner had cut down the tree and built a swimming pool. I did not tell my father. That new owner is long gone now himself. I have never been back inside the house or seen the backyard, but I drive by often. It sits at the top of a hill. When I turn the corner, I slow to a crawl, and try to bring the memories back.

I remember taking shots (which means two people playing hockey) on the driveway with the net against the garage door, or leaving my bicycle against the railing unlocked when I came home for lunch. I like to drive by in early summer, especially, when the grass grows quickly. Someone has almost always just cut their lawn, and I breathe in the scent. It takes me back, almost, to summer nights of playing hide-and-seek with the neighbourhood kids. But this sensation is not complete, and it's fleeting. I can't truly grasp it. It doesn't inhabit me. For a few seconds, I feel a warmth of familiarity, and then the trail goes cold again, as if I am a hunting dog who has lost the scent of the quarry. I don't know what I hope to find, but I keep coming back. In all four seasons, in the morning, at dusk, late at night.

Re: Medals
8/7/2010 6:43 PM
From: mia hakim
To: Ivan Pyefinch

Okay, you can keep the job.
mia

9

Huda, a young woman, visibly moved. Throughout the scene, the camera never leaves her face, no matter who else is talking.

"Too bad that you never got to know him," Huda says. "If so many young Tunisians in Sfax discovered the world through literature and thought, it's because of David and his bookstore, and all the French and Arabic treasures it held. Yes, a good man, and deep, who knew a lot of things."

"They told me that David went to see all the Jews who were left in Sfax, one by one", I say. "He grew sadder each time, and one day he committed suicide by throwing himself down the stairs, at his home."

Huda flashes her eyes at me. "Impossible. I spent nearly all my time with him. David loved life, people, books, cats, and he did not want to die. I told him, if you were Muslim, Mr. David, I would marry you, even if you're seventy-two and I'm twenty-five."

Her eyes water: "It was an accident on the stairs in his house, because of the arthritis in his knees. David was a loyal man. I should have married him. He loved cats. Every morning, he crossed the town for a bag of fish heads, and called all the cats for breakfast. He knew the Quran, how the prophet Himself stayed perfectly still until the cat that was sleeping on his clothes woke up."

The Jewish cemetery in Sfax. The elderly groundskeeper brings us to David's grave. The sound of wind in the Cyprus trees. In my head, I hear the Kaddish, the Jewish prayer for the dead. I leave a stone on the monument. An old cat prowls.

I HAVE no childhood memory of seeing Horace or Aida in a bookstore or even of them reading a book. We had books, yes. Fully unabridged hard covers of novels popular in the 1950s and 1960s, political biographies, and *Reader's Digest* books, which arrived every month as part of the magazine subscription. Each volume contained three or four condensed novels, which Horace must surely have thought was a great deal. We needed somewhere to put them so he built a bookcase into the wall next to my bedroom, which was a few steps from the rec room. On my way to watch television, I would run my fingertips along the covers, the way another boy might run a stick against a white picket fence. Just for the noise of it.

The books remained in shadow, unsought, undusted, fulfilling their purpose by sitting there.

We had the same style of bookcases in the original cottage—recessed into the walls—and more of the same condensed books with paper sleeves or faux leather covers. When Horace built the new addition, he installed still more shelves, fashioning them on his lathe out of his two-hundred-year-old pine from the white garage. They sat on either side of the fireplace and above the space for the television. Here Aida displayed the complete works of Dickens in thirty volumes, as well as two versions of Shakespeare's collected works. She must have picked them up at an auction. Like the baby grand piano no one played that she bought for their house in the country, the books were there to be seen rather than experienced. Maybe they sometimes glanced at the covers during commercials. Aida stored lesser works in the attic or under beds in oily flower boxes. Lurid Perry Mason thrillers by Earle Stanley Gardner, or cheap romance paperbacks that featured on the cover a handsome doctor, an attractive nurse, and a third woman in the distance who harboured some pain and longing in her face.

I EMAIL Mia the translation and then head to the cottage to make Horace and Aida a full breakfast—eggs, pancakes, toast, the works. Horace digs in greedily, while Aida pecks out of politeness, appreciative more of the attention and effort than the result. No matter. My goal is simply to keep them occupied in the cottage until all the neighbours have streamed down the road. They will pass by in clumps, some in cars, but others walking with lawn chairs. A dead giveaway for the annual meeting, which must be avoided at all costs.

"Well that was a good snack, when do we eat?" Horace

says, chuckling.

I've heard this line a hundred times, uttered usually after Aida has slaved for hours over a meal. It's hard to begrudge him, with all the frozen food they've been eating.

I leave Aida to clean up the kitchen and turn on the TV, hoping the latest news will engage Horace. With the aerial, we only get a handful of stations, but thankfully, WWNY from Watertown in New York is coming in strong today.

"*Face the Nation* will be on in a few minutes," I tell him.

"That's right."

As he settles into his armchair, he picks up his latest envelope from the *Reader's Digest* sweepstakes. Bits and pieces of stickers he has to attach to keep in the running for the grand prize fall onto the carpet.

I leave him to help Aida in the kitchen. Down the road, at our treasurer's house, our neighbours will be gathering around the coffee urn from Tim Horton's and fighting good naturedly over the chocolate Timbits. In the few minutes before the meeting is called to order, they'll trade gossip about who is in arrears for the road fee, they'll cluck in sympathy for whoever just went into or got out of hospital, and they'll make nice with the newcomers. Then they will dredge up the question of the road again and, this year, the call of the permanent residents for some form of change may conquer the interests of old-time cottagers like Horace. It's not the humiliation of a defeat for Horace that worries me. It's more how he would react to a loss when he's so used to getting his own way.

THE front door, which is made of glass panes, slams shut. The sound itself makes me jump, but worse, it means that Horace has left the cottage, either in a hurry or without thinking, or both. Normally, afraid that the force of the slam would break the glass, Horace is fastidious about easing the door shut. But, I think, these are no longer normal times.

I follow in his wake toward the garage. If I can hustle him back to the cottage before the stragglers wander down the road, we can still avoid the meeting. Yet halfway across the lawn, just over my dew line, I hear the telltale honk of Margaret's golf cart, which sounds like the goofy horn in Herb Alpert's "Tijuana Taxi." No doubt she has stopped outside the open garage door to chat, as she often does. With her arthritis, she is a familiar enough sight in the cart but not at this hour. Horace may think to ask where she's going, and Margaret may remind him about the road meeting. I can't control every variable, it seems, as hard as I try.

Margaret and her husband Paul are there with her daughter Annabel and their granddaughter Gail, which makes them stand out even more. As they stop in front of our garage, the small Canadian flag on the back of the cart loses wind and collapses. Horace doesn't notice or he would surely show off the no-droop design of his flag on the cliff.

Margaret's parents were the first to buy land here after the war. After her father died and her mother went into long-term care, Margaret and Paul took over the cottage and built a permanent home. They are in their mid-sixties now, although Horace still likes to recall how he once held the newborn Margaret in the palm of his hand. Each time he does, Margaret smiles indulgently at this memory beyond her reckoning. Her daughter Annabel, who is in her thirties, might remember tugging at my leg to play baseball with her brother when she was seven or eight. I don't remind her. To share the memory—the only one of her I have—gives it more importance than it deserves. Or maybe I simply can't reconcile the memory of that girl with the woman who has a daughter of her own. Annabel and her family bought the cottage five doors down that used to belong to my best friend. Although they renovated the property, the exterior remains much the same, including the garden shed. I have a photo of me lying on the roof of the shed from the early 1970s that I would like to show them. I resist because I don't want to become my father, imposing my memories on others at the slightest provocation. The shed is theirs now, and why would they care about my experience? They have their own histories and mythologies to build. One day, long after Margaret, Horace, and probably I have passed away, Gail may take over their cottage or own her grandparents' house. The thought makes me acutely conscious that I have no progeny. Our family's line, and our presence here, ends with me.

"It's a nice morning for a little drive," Margaret says.

Her voice is all sunny, but she throws me a look. She understands the need to keep Horace from the meeting, which irritates and reassures me both. Once she was an ally in keeping the gravel road. Now, as one of the new perms, she has her own agenda.

"Are you coming to the meeting?" says Gail.

She has gone off script, judging from how Annabel pokes her in the side, and the look between her grandparents. Their faces are as crestfallen as their sagging flag.

"What's that?" Horace says. "The road meeting? Is that today?"

Horace notices me standing beside him. His face is twisted in a familiar look of anxiety and confusion, his voice a mix of disbelief and accusation.

"The road meeting is this morning," he tells me. "Did you know that?"

"I'd forgotten."

"Well, Jesus, we've got to go. They'll be trying to pave the road again."

Gail slips off the back seat and comes over to us.

"You can take my seat, Mr. Pyefinch," she says.

"What's she saying?"

"She's saying that Margaret can take you with them on the cart."

"On the what?"

I turn him around so he can see the vacated seat on the back of the cart. I walk him over, helping get over the hump that leads to the road so he doesn't fall backward. He bends awkwardly to sit on the back seat beside Annabel. Then, without the fanfare of the horn this time, they set off down the road at a good clip, kicking up dust and pebbles in their wake. Horace grips the post with his left hand, just below the flag that is now flapping so proudly in the apparent wind. Raising his right arm, he salutes me vigorously with a big grin, unaware of how his elbow has knocked into Annabel.

Gail snickers at the sight.

"That was nice of you to give up your seat," I tell her.

"It's okay. I didn't really want to go."

Gail has the smallest trace of a conspiratorial smile, unable to resist showing me how clever she is. She hasn't learned yet to play completely dumb, but no doubt that will come quickly. She has already mastered the art of getting what she wants while appearing altruistic. No doubt Margaret warned everyone not to talk about the meeting when they saw Horace in the garage, and Gail saw her chance. I'm torn between admiration that someone so young can seize an opportunity and make it work with the knowledge that she has put me in an awkward position.

Gail turns quickly and runs toward her cottage. She keeps to the edge of the grass, to protect her bare feet, the way I once did. I watch until she passes the garden shed and disappears.

—☞ 10 ☜—

I CHECK IN on Aida, although she'll forget everything I say before I'm out the door. She seems comfortable enough with her tea in her habitual spot near the patio window. I've put her decoupage projects within reach—a box of paper butterflies and birds that she cuts out painstakingly for jewel boxes she will never finish. With the meeting starting in ten minutes, and Aida not dressed, there's not much more I can do.

I pocket my Blackberry in case I get mail from Mia. I am starting to wonder what will happen between her and Karim, if they will get together again. There's no clue so far in their scenes together, but she has told me these are mostly imagined. She's gone once to Tunisia for preliminary research, but needs to return again to flesh out a scenario. If she gets funding to write a script, then she'll push for more money to do the actual filming. It may not resemble what she's written.

Maybe Mia's fictional conversations with Karim on the edge of the desert aren't so different from my own talks with Aida. My words seem real, in the moment I speak with her, but then they drift off like so much sand. I'm left wondering if I actually spoke them aloud, and if it would matter if I said other words in their place.

Talking with Horace is different. So much effort to find an oasis—some neutral subject that does not remind him of how the government stole his right to drive. And for what? He will be holding forth now at the doughnut plate, his thoughts uncensored without my intervention. Perhaps I should just let him make his case for the gravel road, one last time, even if he can't vote for his own position. Or else I could let him vote in my stead, even if it's not strictly kosher. Maybe that doesn't matter much either.

Years ago, when Horace and I walked door to door to collect fees to grade the road, he was the one who censored me. I stood beside him with the cookie jar and, at his insistence, kept my mouth shut. He did not want me distracting people from the cause, but my interruptions would not have mattered. The cottage road was our church, and no one refused the collection plate.

We were all so much friendlier back then.

If the potholes got bigger in the off year between gradings, cars simply slowed down, especially after a rain when young boys would bring their boats and trucks to play in the massive puddles. In the face of an oncoming car, one driver would pull off to the grassy shoulder, and the other would raise a finger from the steering wheel to acknowledge the gesture as he passed.

Some of the older residents turned their cottages into permanent homes, but it didn't change how people treated each other. Then strangers began to buy rundown cottages, put up gorgeous new homes, and sell them off to new strangers who sold them for even more. When cars meet now on the road, someone still moves over, but no one lifts a finger. Against the protests of Horace and other old-time cottagers, the perms won the vote to increase the road fees to cover snow plowing. Some cottagers refuse to pay the fees at all, and never show up at the annual meeting. This only plays into the hands of the perms, who are slowly gathering the votes to pave the road.

And I fear that today is the day.

When I arrive at the meeting, Horace is sitting beside Margaret in the circle of chairs they've set up on the lawn. Les, our chair, has already called the meeting to order. A retired manager of the chemical plant near Prescott, he relishes his leadership role in our little world. He waves me into the circle with two impatient strokes of his hand during the review of last year's minutes. Some guy in his forties wearing aftershave and a cashmere sweater draped over his shoulders gives up his seat for me so I can sit beside Horace. I take a quick look around the circle for familiar faces and empty chairs. There's always one person who has died. I start to feel proud that Horace has made it back here, at least one more time. But of the twenty people here, I only know half by sight and a third by name. The rest must be new perms.

Horace seems more focused on removing the liner from his muffin without tearing the paper than listening to the discussion. At first I think he's waiting for debate on the road to start or that, as usual, he has no interest in what other people say. Then I realize he's not wearing his hearing aids. I smile at him encouragingly, but his blank gaze resembles the eyes of a bear. I can't project or predict what he's thinking, and it's dangerous to try.

After the usual complaints about noise and garbage from renters, Les opens the floor to discussion about paving the road. Three of the perms, including Cashmere Man, speak in quick succession as if reciting key messages prepared by a comm team in a government department. A sound investment. Lower maintenance. Easier to plow. Less pollution from dust. I'm surprised they don't try to sell this as our contribution to the low-carbon economy.

Horace has dozed off, his head bowed forward as if in

agreement with Cashmere Man. I want to shake him awake, revive all the self-righteous indignation that I've come to loathe. He needs to stand up and defend our rights before they pave paradise.

"Shall I call for the vote?" Les asks.

"Not yet," I say.

Horace jars awake at the sound of my voice, then closes his eyes again as I pause to think of what to say next. I hear his own voice in my mind. I may not be able to change the vote, but the perms shouldn't have everything their own way.

"You've talked about how the road will be easier to plow in the winter, and that sounds right because this is nothing but a snow job," I tell them. "You're trying to ram this decision through when you know the summer residents don't want to pay for the asphalt. I can name three cottagers who aren't here today. Did they send in proxy votes?"

I pause to catch my breath, hoping my impromptu speech will propel Horace into action. But it's Glen, the treasurer, who speaks first. He's a retired police constable, another guy used to getting his own way.

"We have four proxies, three for and one against, including yours," Glen says. "I hope you don't expect to vote twice."

"You're the treasurer, not the chair," I tell him. "How do you know how people voted?"

Glen clears his throat and pulls himself up straight in his lawn chair.

"This isn't a secret ballot," he says.

"If we pave the road, cars will drive faster, and that makes it more dangerous for my kids," Annabel says. Her parents shift in their chairs, and glance at each other. It's hard to tell if Margaret is embarrassed or angry that Annabel has a different opinion than hers.

A woman I don't know protests that Annabel lives at the end of the road so she's not affected by other cars.

"Yes, but my kids visit their grandparents," Annabel says. "They're running down the road all the time."

"We can put in speed bumps," Glen says. "I'll write up a ticket for anyone who goes too fast. I've still got a book of them somewhere."

That gets Glen a laugh and seems to deflate Annabel, who falls silent.

I look desperately at Horace. Do something, I want to shout. Channel some of that outrage you've reserved for the government that took away your driving licence. Horace is alert now, but says nothing. Les calls for the vote, and it passes fourteen to four, with my proxy, Annabel, and two old-time cottagers as the holdouts. I suspect at least eight cottagers didn't bother to send in a proxy vote. Maybe they would have made a difference.

"I have a statement to make," Horace says.

The victors are too busy congratulating themselves to pay attention to Horace.

"Listen up!" I tell them, my voice raised. "Horace has something to say."

He will put them all in their place—the smug ex-cop, the patronizing ex-manager, the nouveau riche with their aftershave and sweaters and convertibles. He will lecture them on how he was in the war to defend our freedoms, and how today on our little road, it's a dark day for democracy. A tiny minority has manipulated the outcome through collusion, deception, and subterfuge. He never thought he would see the day. The dust stirred up by the gravel in our common road hearkens back to the time of the First Nations people who once travelled along our river in canoes and may well have camped right where we sit today. What's more, the countless bits of stone in the road represent the multitudes of the world. If we pave this road, we are silencing all the dissonant opinions, all the people who don't fit in, all the marginalized and oppressed whose rights are so easily trampled. We will end up with a uniform surface that smooths over difference.

"Listen up!" I repeat, and something in the edge of my voice makes them quiet down.

Horace looks around the room to make sure he has everyone's attention.

"I'm inviting everyone back to see my new air force flag," he says.

 11

AS THE DIAL-UP connection chugs away, slowly revealing images of Mia Hakim I've found on the web, I feel like I'm leaving the home world. Karen doesn't wear makeup or jewellery, unless you count the Rosie the Riveter button pinned to her knapsack—the one where Rosie shows off her bicep with the caption "We Can Do It!" The knapsack, slung over her right shoulder, is empty except for a small change purse and her iPhone. Karen will wear more feminine pants than jeans but never skirts or dresses. If absolutely necessary, she will don a sports bra. For years she has worn her hair in a no-muss no-fuss pageboy with blunt bangs. It's a look she perfected in university, saw no need to change, and to which I became accustomed as my own ideal of beauty.

On Planet Mia, hair is shoulder-length, a mass of curls, and multi-layered strands jut out all over the place. It covers Mia's ears but not the long dangly earrings. She wears three rings on both hands, and at least seven or eight bracelets on each wrist. In one photo, she is wearing leather pants, a blue jean-jacket, and an orange scarf. In another, a frilly skirt with a sensuous top just short of décolleté. In another, an elegant dress that shows off her curves. She has no lipstick, but the corners of each eye have been shaded to match some element of her clothing. I cannot picture her wandering around in any of these ensembles in Tunisia. Maybe this quality of otherness is part of the disconnect she feels going home.

In a working-class neighbourhood overflowing with people, the camera follows and then stops to go elsewhere… toward women wearing the Hijab. Few wear the Niqab and even fewer the Burka.

I notice an incredible diversity, elegance, nonchalance, creativity, and even freedom, in how women wear the veil. It's not uncommon to see two attitudes toward the veil among friends walking arm-in-arm, or in the same workplace, or even in the same family. The rationales for wearing it are above all and most often associated with religion but not always. I've learned a woman will wear a scarf as a fig leaf, hiding white roots or a bad hair day in general. It also depends on her mood and state of mind whether it's worn as a vow, a sign of respect, or a symbol of mourning. Women completely veiled in black are rare.

There are a thousand-and-one ways to wear the veil. Typically, the veiled woman in Tunisia is relatively young, coquettish, and creative, with the scarf affirming her choice to be part of a surprisingly modern nation. After all, women in Tunisia got the vote before women in France. I get the impression that Tunisia is adapting to change freely and with individuality, whereas the veil in Iran or Saudi Arabia remains a constraint imposed by an all-powerful religious state.

IN the 1970s, Horace once applied for a position in Saudi Arabia, where Bell Canada had just won a contract. They planned to send me to a boarding school in Switzerland. We would meet up halfway at Christmas. They were in their fifties then, stuck in the routine of Ottawa-cottage for nearly twenty years. He and Aida had travelled—to Europe for their twenty-fifth wedding anniversary, and to the Bahamas and Florida for holidays. Otherwise, she had rarely left the country. In her mind, the desert offered endless possibility. I can imagine her in the guarded compound, drinking tea with other parched wives to while away the time, unable to leave without an escort. They waited for their husbands to come home from work, counting the days when they could return to Canada with fattened pensions. All those veiled women. Would she envy them their ability to hide in full view?

"They didn't want someone with Horace's skills," Aida had said. After the disdain of the word "skills," her voice had trailed off, as if not certain which way to go.

OUR summer days at the cottage take on a hazy routine. From the guest room at the back of the garage, the texts of Mia Hakim transport me from the edge of the St. Lawrence to the desert of Tunisia and its unnamed sea. I come up with words to capture her tense dialogue with Karim, the attempts to reconcile her postcard memories with the world around her. I wait for the love scene that will surely come. Horace dozes off at all hours, springing awake to complete previously unimagined tasks that suddenly had life-and-death urgency. He kicks the driver's manual out of his way from where it has slipped from his hands onto the rug. A few times a week, we head out for more frozen food, carrot muffins, and memories. Aida sits with her tea and cuttings, or waters the geraniums that sit in pots on top of stone posts along the cliff. The flowers are drowning from all the attention.

Today, Horace is itchy about the house in town where the lawn needs cutting and watering, and so the three of us pile into the Roadmaster. In a clockwise shift in position from my childhood, Aida sits in the back, Horace in the passenger seat and I get behind the wheel.

"You back there, dear?" he says.

"Oh, I'm here all right," Aida answers.

Horace's tone is self-mocking, as is hers, but he raises his hand over his shoulder so Aida can grasp it.

They have lived in the house in town for eight years, ever since moving back permanently from Florida. A small stroke had left him with no ill effects, but he knew it would raise their insurance rates for winters in the States. We've had our fun, he declared. He then packed and drove them back himself, towing the Roadmaster behind a moving van. A few months before 9/11 changed everything, the border guard took one look inside the vacuum-sealed van and waved them through. Only after retrieving their furniture from twenty years of storage did Aida divulge her own crisis: a blood condition that would likely kill her within ten years. Horace seemed more upset about having inadvertently lied on their health insurance forms than with the news his wife had now less than five years to live. But I don't really believe that. His fear often takes the form of anger.

I hold my breath as we approach the house, filled with dread of a break-in. In Florida, although they lived in a gated community, Horace insisted they store Aida's gold charm bracelet in a safe deposit box at the bank. He did the same here. The bracelet holds souvenirs from the trip to Europe for their silver anniversary: a tiny crown, an Eiffel Tower, a French poodle, and a stein, as well as a hollow circle of gold with the number 25 in the middle. It has several sweetheart lockets, empty of tiny photos, as well as other trinkets purchased on vacations abroad, including a St. Christopher medallion that reads, "Look at me and be safe." My favourite pieces, the ones that capture Aida's essence, the ones I can see her buying with sheer, but restrained, delight are the thimble and the teapot.

My tension is less about what anyone could take, and more about how Horace would react to the affront of intruders. Years ago, thieves were in and out of our house in Ottawa within fifteen minutes, the time it took to exchange a defective sprinkler at Canadian Tire. They had dumped all the drawers on the beds, running away with eighty dollars before they heard the Country Squire pull into the driveway. But Horace didn't dwell on the good timing that scared them off or the stock certificates they didn't take. He didn't even let Aida clean up the mess. Instead, he muttered under his breath as he stuffed his underwear and socks back into the drawers, hatching a plan for revenge. He figured these bad eggs, or some of their ilk, might come back. Rather than get better locks on the windows, he tried to attract thieves by making the house look empty. With Aida and me at the cottage for the summer, he left the grass hay-like in the backyard, piled newspapers on the front porch like an overzealous paperboy, and turned the lights off at night. Then he slept in a pup tent in the backyard with a baseball bat.

For years later, each time we came back from the cottage he grew tenser as we approached home. Within the last block, he would unclip his seatbelt, ready to dash out to grab the ne'er do wells. As we drove up the hill, he stared at our house until it came fully into view, expecting to see a flash of clandestine movement. He would accelerate as he turned the corner, screech to a halt in the driveway, and then fly out the door around the side of the house into the backyard. Aida and I were expected to stay in the station wagon until he gave the All-Clear, but eventually I went around the other side of the house, just in case they outsmarted him. Horace and I met up at the apple tree to compare notes. I felt a strange combination of exhilaration, fear, relief, and pride.

Even if no one has bothered any of their properties since, I feel that ancient rise of adrenaline in the home stretch. It's a corner lot with roads on two sides and an open backyard. No place to hide. There could no safer place on the street, really. Even so I had put sticks in the windows to reinforce the locks and set up three lights on timers. Far from being grateful, Horace was puzzled by these precautions. We lock the door, he'd said.

Look at me and be safe.

I want to believe his dissipating fears represent the wisdom of old age rather than a sign of forgetfulness. Whatever the reason, I more than make up for his missing anxiety. Just as he once did, I speed up as I turn onto their street. Any second now I'll see someone running out with their scratched-up copy of Herb Alpert's *Whipped Cream and Other Delights* or maybe with Horace's auxiliary toolbox from the garage. But Horace points to the community mailbox up ahead, a command to pull over before we reach the house. I could explain why we should go to the house first, but this would only stoke up old fears for nothing. I try to quell my own anxiety, tapping the steering wheel rather than gripping it tightly as he gets out of the car.

From here I can glimpse the homemade trailer on the driveway, its tongue propped up on a two-by-four so any rain can pour out the open back. Horace lumbers out of the passenger seat with difficulty as I've parked too close to the curb. He points at the mailbox, dropping his finger down two rows and three across to the right to find his spot, or perhaps thinking the pointing gesture will, like me, obey his command. He fumbles with the keys, first to get them out of his pocket, and then to find the right one. It's all I can do not to abandon him by the side of the road, run to the house, and check all the windows and doors.

He flings the mail onto the dashboard, which falls onto my feet, before manoeuvring himself onto the seat. I pick up the envelopes from the floor mat, blanching at the sight of a Ministry of Transport letter addressed to Aida. Her doctor must have asked them to cancel her driver's licence. A relief, for me, but it will jumpstart Horace's protests just when I had him relatively calmed down.

"What are we doing here?" Aida asks, and I don't know what to answer.

The only assault on their dignity is the stale air that greets us when we open the front door. St. Christopher, or the Creator Himself, has protected them once again. There's no point in airing the place out for a few hours, especially since they never open the windows anyway. Instead I set up Aida in the sunroom with a cup of tea and her butterfly clippings. I didn't think to bring fresh milk so I open a new can of Carnation. When I pass by the south side with the mower I will be able to look in on her through the patio door in case her blood takes this moment to curdle.

Fifteen years after her ten-year death sentence, Aida has so far beat the odds. Yet I wonder how much the stress of keeping her illness a secret poisoned her mind. The shock of the cold and snow couldn't have helped, nor Horace's obsession with the missing shutters on their new home either. He spent their first winter with a pile of papers on the dining room table to prepare his court case against the developer. A matter of principle, he said. Was his indignation a distraction from the Ontario winter and Aida's growing confusion and depression? Is that what caused the intolerable itch on his back?

When spring came, their moods seemed to improve. Although Aida had lost interest in cooking, she still accompanied Horace to the grocery store. The defeat in court behind him, Horace was bent on replacing the aging septic tank at the cottage with a homemade oil drum. It just needed a baffle to separate the solids, but he couldn't figure out how to attach it. Unlike the air force flag, it needed to flap.

"Sounds like a baffling problem," I told him.

Horace grinned like I knew he would. It was the first time a problem had ever stumped him, but surely he couldn't be an expert in everything. He was fine. They would both enjoy summer at the cottage as they always did. The sunshine would do wonders for them. I'm surprised I didn't tell them to drink lots of orange juice, the way Aida would do for me.

The guy at the demolition company rigged up the baffle for him as a favour. All Horace had to do was pick it up with the trailer. I was relieved, even as I questioned the legality of the septic tank switcheroo. We weren't in the 1950s anymore. There were strict bylaws now, rules and regulations, and inspectors. Yet his determination to sidestep these minor details was perversely reassuring. If he was still belligerent, then he had to be okay. Nor did I worry about this trip into the countryside. He had been hauling that trailer forever, sometimes with me and my friends in the back to give us a thrill on the gravel road at the cottage. He had built it from scratch and installed all the brake lights himself. I had seen him parallel park with the damned thing in tow, while as a sixteen-year-old I couldn't back it up without forking.

"Just do the opposite of what you think is right," he'd said.

So I had turned the wheel left when I wanted the trailer to go right. Simple enough.

"Now you've got it," he'd said.

It was one of those rare moments when I felt neither superior nor inferior. Just equal, which was all I ever wanted.

Horace had driven back and forth to the demolition site without incident. Yet, as he told me later, he had trouble backing up with the trailer.

"The fellow did it for me," he'd remarked, chuckling. "I guess I'd never done it before."

I couldn't decide which was worse—his loss of the skill itself or the memory of ever having it. His itch started up again, and Aida stopped her shopping trips, preferring to stay home in her bathrobe. I contacted the geriatric outreach team, who had them both do the clock test, and neither could draw hands to indicate the time. The team put them on some meds, and the Ministry of Transport took away his driver's licence. If he passed this special test with the occupational therapist, he had a fighting chance to drive again. For Horace, fighting chances were the best kind.

"If you hadn't got the government involved, I'd still be driving," he had said. "There's nothing wrong with my head. It's just the damned itch. It's driving me crazy."

I GET the mower out, while Horace looks for a place to plant the hollow pipe to hold his flag. Inside the double-car garage, sealed boxes from storage marked "Junk" have somehow gravitated into the space where they normally parked their car in winter. Dead centre, the oil drum with its custom-made baffle waits for Horace. I expect he wants to drive it up himself triumphantly when they return his licence, backing the trailer through our narrow front gate like nobody's business.

I make long passes on the lawn, shooting cuttings away from where Horace is kneeling in the rock and flower garden. It only takes a moment to stick the pipe in the ground, but he lingers. Maybe he's imagining how the flag will command the respect of neighbours and passersby. I see it more as a talisman, drawing in mean-spirited pirates on Halloween night. Bored with smashing pumpkins and stealing plastic grave markers, they will spray paint a skull-and-crossbones over the British ensign.

Each time I round the corner of the house I check on Aida in the sunroom. *Don't be so hard to get along with.* A pet phrase of hers. She certainly makes it easy for all of us. I can park her in any chair with a cup of tea, and attend to her demanding husband at will. This time, though, she's nowhere in sight. My instinct to expect the worst was one of Karen's habitual complaints, and I try hard to come up with innocent explanations. She may have gone to the bathroom or to the kitchen for more tea. Perhaps down to the basement where she has reams of half-started decoupage projects. Maybe to the bedroom for a nap. I could leave it at that, continue the mowing and breathe into my anxiety as Karen used to push me to do. Instead I can't resist peering through the window of the sliding door. Beyond the kitchen table I glimpse Aida in a heap on the linoleum floor. I try the door, forgetting it's double-locked. Shutting off the mower, I run round to the front. Horace is nowhere in sight either, but I can only handle one worst-case scenario at a time.

She is back in her chair, with her butterfly clippings. Did I dream the whole thing? No, I can see where the mug of tea has exploded in the microwave and dripped onto the counter and floor. The scatter rug in front of the sink is askew. Either one could have caused her to slip.

"How are you doing?" I ask her.

"Oh, I'm fine. Working away."

"Would you like some tea?"

"That's a good idea."

She gets up, favouring her left leg.

"You're limping. Are you okay?"

"I must have bumped into something."

"Let me bring you the tea."

She returns to her chair without a protest.

Outside the lawn mower roars back to life, and Horace pushes through the rows I had abandoned, taking care not to get entangled by the extension cord. I leave him to it, and sit down to spend time with Aida. But what could I ask her now that she could answer? I'm too late.

When did silence become her language? Did it open up space for the depression or was it the other way around? It's harder than ever to get a fix on Aida. She spoke rarely of her life, and unlike Horace, offered no grand narrative. The more shards of her past I conjure up, the less I can fit her into a single image. Pictures take shape as if I witness them, and past and present blend with the efficiency of a MixMaster.

Aida had no past before I was born. I was certain of this. And when I started to think otherwise, I never dared probe her silence. Even when she wasn't at the sewing machine, her back toward me, her mouth was full of pins that muffled her voice and threatened to pierce me if I got too close. Like Horace, she did not fit easily into a parental role, and I never felt comfortable calling her Mom or Mother. The terms evoked a particular form of intimacy we did not share. Ours was a relationship based on fragile collusion—an unspoken agreement to prop up Horace's grandiosity and to suffer from it. Our arrangement was fragile because Aida wanted to be the greater martyr, and was willing to punish me for the privilege.

We were uneasy allies, both of us hiding in silence broken only by her pet phrases.

Don't get overheated. The meaning of this danger zone, and what might happen if I reached it, was unspoken. Maybe she didn't know herself. I imagined a feverish state brought on by too much excitement and pleasure—an excess of emotion. Silence as precaution. I made up rules I thought would please her, kept my demeanour cool and unthreatening, doused any fire in a wet blanket to keep her own temperature from rising unnaturally. Not too hot, not too cold—I strived to be tepid.

Who was your servant last year? Her tone was self-deprecating, as if she didn't mind waiting on us. But she must have longed to be served just once as she plied her face with creams to ward off aging, to be the fairest of them all.

Don't forget your pills. The past was forbidden, the future to be tamed. A message to herself, as well as me. She kept them in the cupboard above the circular dishwasher, a space-age appliance that needed a push to gain momentum, as if the dishes were children on a faulty merry-go-round. Steam rising through the poor seal made her face sweat, counteracting the benefit of the estrogen. My antibiotics worked, though, repressing the natural aspects of adolescence.

Silence as obligation, a wifely duty: she was a sounding board, offering unwanted suggestions or slipping into a private realm to keep the world at bay. I stood at Horace's side while he worked on his lathe, and she suddenly appeared. *Go and play.* I rarely protested much, choosing instead to slink away. I was determined not to cause her any more grief. I resented her intrusive helpfulness, for giving me the freedom I craved but couldn't take for myself.

Silence was her weapon of choice, sharper than any sword, less forgiving than the back of a hand, more accurate than a guided missile. It said nothing, and so, everything. The wrong word or opinion could reveal ignorance. *You know Horace.* She let him do the talking, and that too embarrassed her. How to rein him in, and yet stay protected? She spoke in asides, sandwiching her silence with playful yet pointed jabs. Her eyes fell into a deeper void.

Silence as concealment: the Jehovah's Witnesses rang the doorbell, and she made me lie on the floor next to the chesterfield while she stayed in the kitchen. Her good manners would keep the proselytizers at the door until they decided to leave. Maybe she would be obliged to invite them in for tea, and then would worry the neighbours would think she had *got religion.* I held my breath, waiting for the sound of the chimes to fade. *I find it hard to believe in a hereafter.* I wanted to know what she believed, to become the witness she couldn't hide from.

Now she has a whole new set of phrases that with each repetition lose what little meaning they convey.

We're in our eighties now. We never celebrate her birthday, not the way she does ours. I didn't know the date, not for years. Horace liked to say that life with him was the greatest gift she could have. She did not protest. Silence as armour, deflecting hurt.

Is silence really an oasis for her? Maybe it's the desert, an arid patch that grows, filled with regrets and loss, eroding her mind. Lest she get overheated, she uses words to convince herself otherwise. *We've had a good life.*

I HEAR the silence outside, uncertain how long it's been there. Then I hear the crash of the garage door as it reaches the driveway, signalling that Horace is ready to go home. I'm guessing the oil drum is still where he left it.

And then he arrives, sweaty, glowing, trailing cut grass that has got wrapped up in his pant cuffs. He throws himself into one of the armchairs opposite Aida.

"You're sleeping on the job," he says. "I had to finish cutting your lawn."

My lawn? He has a chuckle in his voice that blunts the habitual sharpness of his tone. Maybe there was always soft humour and I'm only hearing it now.

"What's this?" he says.

The mail. I had brought it in, then left it on the coffee table. I should have thrown it on the lawn and cut it into shards with the mower.

"A lot of junk," I tell him.

"There's something here from the government."

He tears it open, scanning it quickly. I wait for his skeptical face to snarl into a rant against the government that's now taking away his wife's right to drive. All because of her no-good doctor. But he cocks his head slightly. His eyes narrow in curiosity and then widen.

"They want her to write a driving test in the fall," he says. "That means she can drive right now. We should test her going home."

He thrusts the letter at me for confirmation.

For once I want Horace's mind to be muddled, but he's right. Every two years after the age of eighty, the department makes drivers write a multiple-choice test and take part in a group discussion. Aida will be eighty-four in December. I had wanted her to coast to the end of her driving career, but now I have to bring it to a screeching halt.

"This will solve all our problems until I get my licence back," Horace says. He's jumped up from the chair, pacing around the room as if delivering an impassioned lecture to a skeptical audience. "Why the hell not?"

He looks my way more for confirmation than permission. It would be so easy to give her the keys and avoid another conflict with him. Do the opposite of what you think is right.

"I don't think it's a good idea," I tell him. "Aida fell in the kitchen while we were outside. She's hurt her leg."

"You fell?"

"Oh no, I'm fine."

"She's fine. What the hell are you talking about? Let's try her out right now."

I take her half-finished cold tea, and watch her get up from the corner of my eye. She limps, right on cue, her injury a prop in my campaign to keep them safe.

"Jesus, what's wrong with your leg?"

"I must have bumped it."

Horace falls into the armchair, not with his usual forceful abandon but rather from exhaustion. He struggles for a breath, as if the rapid shift from hope to despair has weakened the air pressure in the room. Is it the knowledge of Aida's fall, her growing confusion, or the disruption to his plans that have sent him crashing to Earth?

"You'll be taking your special test in a few days," I tell him. "Then we'll see what happens."

He shakes his head in disbelief as he pushes himself up from the arms of the chair. He breezes by Aida with his forceful stride, the tail wind nearly knocking her over again.

12

I want to discover the hidden face of this dictatorship that has made women wear the veil again and thrown journalists and lawyers into prison, that buys votes and erases History and the liberal gains of the Republic of Bourguiba, pushing more and more young people into exile toward francophone regions like France and Quebec.

I decide nothing in advance. Once I get there to do research, I know I will find other deserts, other streets, other trees, and other friends than the ones in my heart. I will also need to accept encounters with people who question my motives. Because I can't understand how this country, once a secular republic and a shining light in the Arab world, has become a dictatorship. And how these women, intellectuals, and artists are losing their rights. I want to slip into meetings of writers, poets, and students, both in university settings and underground, and fill my head with their slogans.

I am not leaving empty-handed. I will bring with me this feeling, still new, of security and belonging that surprises me each time I leave, and return, to Montreal. But this time I'm not leaving for a vacation in France. I'm not a tourist standing on the firm earth in search of cultural discovery, but rather in the quicksand of my origins, riding the backwash of my memories.

No one talked politics, religion, independence, tradition, heritage, culture, or exile with a child. They tore me away from a language, a music, a landscape. In their place, they left questions that I have studied, reflected upon, and followed up. From afar. From here.

I will unfold these old questions and throw them in the face of the present, where they will either skip along the surface of water that is all too real or ricochet with a splash into the abyss. All to see if the images that gave them birth have the allure of postcards or not.

These questions, which acted like a railing to keep me safe, will be seen now from the other side—through the eyes of the children of today that I will film.

I will film almost everything, what I chance upon and what I've forgotten; my friends from afar encountered again in Tunisia to bring my invented memories face-to-face with this new reality; all the meetings missed, begun, or impossible; the safe havens of creative spaces, the gestures of artists. But also the inevitable tensions, the rage, the looks of silence that I must interpret.

New questions
8/16/2010 7:18 PM
From: mia hakim
To: Ivan Pyefinch

Dear Ivan,

I have been thinking about that tree in the backyard of your childhood home. Why did you not tell your father it was chopped down?

mia

Re: New questions
8/17/2010 8:32 AM
From: Ivan Pyefinch
To: mia hakim
    I probably feared he would blame me for bringing the bad news. But here's the funny thing: once we moved, he forgot all about his offer to tend the apple tree. He never once spoke about it. I carry the memory on his behalf.
    IP

ON the morning of the driver's test, Horace is turning over pillows and papers in search of his wallet. Aida is helping with the search, but can't retain what she's looking for. Her leg is already much better, as if the fall never happened. I watch the scene with a growing sense of nervous energy. But we're running late for the trip to Smiths Falls. I've never been to the hospital before and need to give myself extra time. Unlike Horace who can misplace his wallet, a tool, or a grocery list but never gets lost on the road, I have a poor sense of direction.

"You don't really need it right now, Horace," I say. "They won't ask for your health card."

"I don't care about that. I want my licence. If I pass this test, I want to drive back."

I should be relieved at this sudden deference to authority, but even if he passes the test today he has so many more hoops to jump through.

"What is it you're looking for, dear?"

"My wallet, goddamn it."

As a child, I was always finding things for Horace. I would dearly love to produce his wallet to see that look of gratitude and relief in his face. I check his pants on the back of the bedroom door, reaching deep into the pocket like I'm fishing out my bag of silver dollars from the old tree. Sure enough my fingers brush up against the worn leather. I pull out the wallet triumphantly and he takes it from my hand without a word, as if it were all meant to be.

"Jesus, look at the time. We've got to get going. Where's my Bible now?"

"That miniature one?" I say. "The one that's not in your shirt pocket?"

A chuckle eases his tension. This small Bible has been kicking around the cottage for years. I've never seen him read it. Obviously, he wants to bring some of the Creator's energy into the test room with him. Either that or he's slipped some rules of the road in between the commandments.

He puts on good shoes, which pinch his toes and make him walk awkwardly. His halting gait, however, is not enough to disturb his hair. He must have given it a second blast with the spray to hold it in place. I hope the chemicals didn't catch the hearing aids, which he has agreed to wear. I've assured him they won't hold his hearing loss against him. If the ministry gives extra points for effort, Horace should pass the test handsomely.

He's quiet as we head to Brockville to find Highway 29 into Smiths Falls. It's a secondary road, and we're stuck behind a farmer's tractor for a few minutes.

"Jesus, just pass this guy, would you?"

The farmer takes the turnoff for Athens, allowing us space to make up for lost time. Once in Smiths Falls, I splurge on parking in the paid lot, and rush after Horace who is stumbling toward the main entrance. We're only a few minutes late, and the occupational therapist—a middle-aged woman with an English accent—doesn't seem bothered. Her accent spurs Horace to talk about his war-time experience in Scotland, but she steers him politely yet decisively to a desk before he can tell her about his friend Bob. As she turns to head back to the front of the room, he grabs her arm.

"Listen to this," he says.

He pulls out his Bible and starts reading from Genesis. She looks my way, and I shrug, determined not to defend or explain Horace. Mostly because I can't. Even I, who thought I knew Horace inside-out, am at a loss to explain this sudden interest in scripture, and how it's going to help with the outcome of the driver's test. Maybe he wants to show her he's a God-fearing man and a good Christian. She adjusts the glasses on her nose, takes a step back, and crosses her arms. Without warning, just after God called the light day, Horace stops reading and turns the book toward the woman.

"Look at the size of that print. Don't even need glasses."

"That's very good, Mr. Pyefinch. If you're ever called to read the Bible on the road, you'll be in fine shape. So as long as you don't try to read and drive at the same time."

Her tone is English-dry, and Horace isn't quite sure if she's making fun of him. I'm sure, though. My instinct to protect him is starting to kick in. In my book, I'm the only one who gets to criticize or ridicule him, and never to his face.

"So when do we do the driving test?" he asks.

"The first step is a written test. I'm going to play a video that will present different situations that you could encounter on the road. You will be presented with five choices for a response, from a to e. You will hear them spoken aloud by the narrator in the video, and they are also written down on the paper I'm about to give you. You will circle what you consider to be the best response. Are we ready?"

Her voice is hypnotic, and even I'm lulled by it. Horace, though, looks at me completely baffled.

"She's going to show a video up there on the TV," I tell him. "It will show you different problems you might come up against when you're driving. They help you out by suggesting five different things you can do. You have to choose what you think is the best one. You circle what you think is the best answer on the sheet."

"Where is this sheet of paper?"

I motion toward the woman to bring him the sheet. Far from being grateful at my plain language intervention, her face has grown colder and sterner. They make a good pair, the two of them. Both so sure of themselves and what they do.

"Do you have another sheet?" I ask. "I'd like to do it as well."

She places my sheet face down on a desk a few over from Horace. Reasserting control of her domain, or maybe she thinks I'll pass him the answers if I sit too close.

The situations come up quickly on the screen, just as they would on the road, and the choices for action are subtle. Worse, the narrator has an English accent and uses convoluted language.

I glance over at Horace, who seems confident marking up the page. Maybe the lessons of the handbook seeped into his brain despite his semi-conscious state in the armchair at the cottage. Twenty minutes later, she picks up our tests. Horace thrusts his paper toward her chest in disgust.

"They don't give you time to think," he says.

"The situations are actually quite indicative of those you are likely to encounter."

"So when do we take the real driving test?"

But she's already turned toward her desk, unwilling to explain the process again.

Horace looks at me helplessly. I could interpret for him, but there's no point. What's done is done, and all of my fantasies for a happy ending are slipping away.

She hands my results back first. Eighty-five percent, which she says is a high score. But, she adds, it also means that fifteen times out of a hundred I would have broken the law or had an accident. I am so afraid for Horace. It will be a long drive home.

Horace fails but only barely. Taking pity on him, the woman gives him another chance: take six driving lessons, and with the recommendation of the instructor, come back for a road test. She provides the names of two driving schools in Brockville that they deal with regularly.

All in all, this could qualify as another of Horace's miracles. Yet he takes it all in stride. Maybe a lifetime of miracles has made him blasé. They have come to be expected. He has never been left forsaken. I think of Aida waiting at home, and wonder if she's okay. I think of Karen playing her heart out in a tiny Ottawa club. I think of Mia being ripped from her family in Tunisia into a life that I still know nothing about.

Horace pounds his chest with two fists for her benefit.

"Hard as a rock."

He heads for the door without another word. It's left for me to thank the woman for her flexibility. I run down the corridor in time to hear his strategy for success.

"I just guessed at the answers," he says. "I circled anything."

He has every reason to maintain his buoyant mood, but by the time we reach the car he is cursing the government again for putting stones in his path at every turn.

"Driving lessons! She probably gets a whatever from the instructors."

"A kickback?"

"Yes, I'd like to kick back, but what can I do? You've got

the car."

I turn the wrong way, as I so often do, even in a familiar neighbourhood. Before he notices my confusion, I pull a U-turn, skidding on to the shoulder of the road, kicking up dust.

"What the hell are you doing?" he says. "The road is that way."

He thrusts his hand in front of my face and I follow his outstretched finger to get home.

⟡ 13 ⟡

The tree of knowledge
8/18/2010 11:46 AM
From: mia hakim
To: Ivan Pyefinch
Dear Ivan,

    I wonder what it has been like for you, carrying this tree in your heart all these years for your father, knowing that he does not remember it. It makes sense to me that you have never looked into the backyard of your old house. So as long as you don't know for certain, the apple tree might still be there. Once you know something you cannot unknow it. I begin to question whether I have the courage to return to Tunis, to witness the absence.

    mia

I am afraid to see our house on the Avenue Al-Djazira turned into a tuna-canning factory and to find the aroma of roasted chestnuts that followed me home from school has been replaced by the acidic smell of fish.

I imagine entering the hall of the building on Avenue de Paris, where the rest of our family lived, and discovering I'm afraid to slide down the leather banister and jump off to the marble steps.

More fears: running onto the lookout until I reach the iron-clad window where I will no longer see the smile of my great grandmother, pushing my nose against the shop window of the *Comptoir des Elégantes* in the hopes of seeing my aunt Zelda, her painted eyelashes, and her cigarette holder.

It's not completely true that I've never been back. Twenty years after I left, I returned for four days to shoot several scenes for a film. But I stayed in a strange neighbourhood that had no connection to my past. I kept alive the idea I would return in search of lost time, the traces that inhabit my memory and shape my identity. Once, on a break, I asked the driver to take me to the souk where I could buy a chickpea soup. I spoke to him in Arabic. He asked why I pretended not to know the language. I'm not pretending, I said, the words surfaced on their own from the back of my head into my mouth. He said I should become a *déguéza*—a fortune teller. He put the scarf on my head because even sorcerers are burned by the sun.

◈ 14 ◈

HORACE DOESN'T like the sound of the two driving schools on the list the woman gave him. They have receptionists that he can't understand. He gets a better feeling from the guy he finds in the Yellow Pages who answers his own phone. David runs a school near the A&W in Brockville, and so we arrange to meet him there in the parking lot the next day. Horace prepares by gathering up copies of letters to the editor, photos of him and his friend Bob in their cadet uniforms, and the story of his infamous spin from ten thousand feet just before the war ended.

"I want to show him the kind of man I am."

DAVID, who seems to be in his mid-forties, is the kind of driving instructor who sports a red t-shirt with the slogan "In my defense I was left unsupervised" to his first meeting with potential clients. I'm almost more irritated by the American spelling than the party-hard message more suited to a twenty-year-old. His attire shows off the tattoos of a mythical water creature on his left arm and a whale on the other, the flipper curling around his muscled bicep. If Horace notices—and I don't see how he can miss them—it doesn't faze him. Not like the image of the silver dollar I had seared onto my skin that unleashed his friend Bob from the deep.

David nods approvingly and maintains eye contact as Horace hands him the package.

"I'll be sure to have a look at this," he says.

His words are enough to win over Horace, who seems ready to write him a cheque on the spot, right on the hood of the Roadmaster.

"So you need six lessons," David says. "We could do three a week. Then I'll be out of your hair in two weeks, and you'll be ready for your test. How does that sound?"

Horace breaks into a wide grin, and looks my way for affirmation. But as much as I would like the lessons to be over with quickly, it feels too easy.

"You'll need to provide a report to the hospital," I tell him.

David waves me off with a hand that says "Pshaw" but is probably more like "Piss off."

"You ready, Horace?" he says. "We can start right now. No, no, in my car over here."

"He's got a special car," I tell him. "It's got a brake on the passenger side."

"Your son's a smart cookie, Horace."

He walks Horace to the driver's side of his Chevy Malibu, rolls back the seat to maximum, and then plants him inside.

"So what's the first thing you need to do?" David says.

"Seatbelts."

"Good man."

David turns to me, his face still a mask of forced joviality, but his left hand carries Horace's precious envelope like it was a loaf of stale bread.

"We'll be back in an hour," David says.

"*Inshallah.*"

He looks at me strangely. The Arabic word emerged on its own from the back of my head and into my mouth, as if it were my language. I had better wait in the A&W before the beating sun scorches my bald spot.

 15

They say that every adopted child wants to see its mother again one day to soothe the ache, and let it fully accept its new family.

If, over there, I become afraid of future memories that will be difficult to accept, I will remember when I left France for

Montreal, at my own bidding this time, a chosen exile. But this is not entirely true either. Because I engineered my exile from the womb of Tunisia, leaving my father and his new wife behind so I could find my mother in France. There was no time to gather memories, and I wanted to forget. This time I will make provisions for the sounds of the dawn, the breath of the wind, the laughter of the desert, the water in the tea, the bare footsteps treading on the path, the shouts from the back alleys, the echo of calls from the courtyards.

I will transcribe faithfully the words of my friends and of their enemies.

On the morning of the last day, at dusk, I will bring back the chants of the poets, but even more, the whisperings of the unknown.

Re: Future Memories
8/20/2010 9:56 AM
From: Ivan Pyefinch
To: mia hakim

Dear mia,
I have tried to transcribe faithfully, but I understand less and less. Strangely, it does not seem to matter. I have spent years translating words and with you it's the space between the words that seems more important.
Ivan

—◦◎◦ 16 ◦◎◦—

I'VE TAKEN to bringing Aida with us to the driving lesson, the two of us waiting in a booth with a frosted mug of A&W root beer while David puts Horace through the paces. The placemat features shameless black and white photos from the 1950s to conjure warm memories of the drive-in experience, the kind we had at the franchise on the highway at the east end of Brockville before they tore it down. The era of car hops on roller skates was already over. Our server, clad in an orange uniform, would walk in sneakers down the cement aisle that divided the facing cars. Like everyone else, we ate in our car with the tray of food resting on the half-opened window on the driver's side. We were the picture-perfect family with Horace ordering a Papa Burger, Aida the Mama Burger and me the Teen Burger, although my voice hadn't begun to change yet. After we finished, Horace would put on our lights again for service, and the car hop would skip down the aisle for our tray and the few coins Horace had left for a tip. He'd back out of the angled spot quickly, as if nothing could get in his way.

"Do you remember all the times we went to the A&W on the highway?" I ask Aida. "After, we would go to Dairy Queen for dessert. It was right across the road."

"Of course I do. All those times."

But I know it's not true, so for my sake as well as hers I don't press. I am so desperate to connect with Aida that I will hold on to her imagined memories and embellish them as my own.

I wonder if Mia ever found her mother in France. Did they sit in rattan chairs on a terrasse in Paris, sipping from espressos as they caught up with each other's lives? Maybe they walked along the Seine with gelatos in shimmering heat, taking jabs at each other as they caught drips with their tongues.

Horace and David are back from the lesson a little early. They're sitting in the car, and I half expect to see the lights come on, as if they want me to trot out at their bidding. But Aida and I are finished anyway so I gather up our stuff, taking one last look at the nostalgic placemat now dampened with root beer rings. I wave at Horace as I get Aida into the Roadmaster. In a few moments he will throw himself into the seat and recount what he's learned with the eagerness of a first grader. I think of all the times I held back my enthusiasm, believing, rightly or wrongly, that Horace would not be interested in my day at school. Was it strength or weakness on my part? All I know is that Horace needs to be heard. He will pout or lash out otherwise.

Today, Horace is uncharacteristically quiet as he leans against the Chevy. It's David who speaks up, clamping his hand on Horace's shoulder.

"We've decided to call it a day with the lessons," David says.

"That's right," Horace says. "We're all done here."

"That's great, Horace," I say. "Aida's already in the car. I just want to talk to David a minute."

"Remember what I told you, Horace," David says, as Horace walks away. "Stay off the highway!"

I wait for Horace to reach the car before facing David.

"So what's going on?" I ask. "Why are you stopping at five lessons?

"No worries. I'll tell them he had the six. They won't know the difference."

"I don't understand why…"

"Because we had a close call today, all right? On the on-ramp to the 401. He got caught alongside two transports, and he couldn't merge. I had to brake for him, and we ended up on the shoulder."

"Why were you taking him on the 401 at all?"

"To scare the bejesus out of him so that if he does get his licence back he won't go on the highway."

"Lesson Five: give the client a near-death experience."

David smirks, but I don't let it go. I'm sure he was spelling licence with an "s" in his head.

"So why stop at five lessons?"

"You couldn't pay me enough to get into a car with him again."

"But you're going to write a report that says he's good to go."

"He deserves another shot, don't you think? As long as he stays off the 401, he should be good for another few years."

"But you won't drive with him."

"What the fuck do you want from me?"

He doesn't wait for an answer, turning instead to the driver's seat of his car where he adjusts the seat forward in one vigorous motion. I could get in the passenger seat beside David, hold the brake pedal down. Better to let him go, count our blessings. Maybe he was right to teach Horace through fear. It's a language he understands. Horace once held me over the cliff to show me it was dangerous. Even today, when I get close to the edge, my breathing gets shallow, which seems to muddy my thoughts. I remember the sensation, my legs kicking out, searching for the firm earth that wasn't there. I can see it happening sometimes, although I'm on the outside looking in, as if it's happening to someone else. Sex with Karen could be like that, too.

DAVID is good to his word because the occupational therapist calls the next day.

"He hasn't followed the template for the report, which doesn't surprise me," she says. "It's why I didn't recommend him. But from the hasty note that he has written, I gather he believes your father is ready for the test. It so happens I have a cancellation tomorrow morning. I'm leaving on holidays after, and then it's booked into November. Did you want to take it?"

Horace is still not quite himself so it might be better to wait. But three months? He will have forgotten everything he's learned, including his fear. There might be snow. And if I delay, if I show anything less than full confidence in Horace, it might send the wrong signal.

"We'll be there."

I put on a big smile for Horace to hide my own misgivings. He's lucid enough, though, to be worried.

"Tomorrow? Jesus wept."

"It's either that or November. And I know how much you've been wanting to get your licence back. This is your chance."

"I don't know."

"See how you feel tomorrow. We can always cancel."

And if we do, he can kiss his chances goodbye. Maybe that's for the best. I don't want him on the road and I won't let Aida drive either. Either of the cab companies would be happy to sell him some chits. I'll put on Herb Alpert's "Tijuana Taxi" and hope the warm memories evoked by the song carry over into real life.

Coffee?
9/2/2010 2:42 PM
From: Karen Bailey
To: Ivan Pyefinch

Hey Nowhere Man,
    I imagine you are up at the cottage for the long weekend.

Are you around next week?
The B****

When Karen and I were hunting for our first apartment I kept finding things wrong with every place—too dark, too grubby, too expensive, too noisy, too insecure. She took to calling me the "Nowhere Man". Later, when she decided I could never commit to our relationship either, she would sing a few bars of the Beatles' song to silence me during arguments. It became a running joke as I counteracted with "The Bitch is Back", a song from Elton John, one of her childhood heroes. Our proxies would fight for us, hurling lyrics into the space between us, until we collapsed in laughter. Often we made love after, turning any residual anger into something more tender.

I haven't heard from Karen in five months. How much do I read into this unexpected overture? Is she trying to say she wants to come back? Do I tell her that I'm unable to see her because I'm at the cottage, taking care of Horace and Aida? This will only confirm to her that nothing has changed; she remains a secondary priority. But how could she be otherwise. She left me, after all. I don't write back right away. Deflect, put off.

Coffee?
9/2/2010 2:50 PM
From: mia hakim
To: Ivan Pyefinch

Dear Ivan,
I am coming to Canada in November, mostly to be in Montreal, but I will be in Ottawa for a day. We can meet for coffee, if you like. I would like to drive by your childhood home. It will be a repetition for my trip to Tunis.
mia

Mia is thinking "repetition" in English means "rehearsal," but maybe she's not far wrong. Driving by the old house countless times is more about repetition than anything else. Then again, I've never done it with anyone sitting beside me so the experience would be new. Eventually, she will want to know something more about me. I swallow hard at the thought. Mia is no longer the stranger on the airplane hearing my life story. She has followed me from the luggage carousel to the taxi stand, and we're sharing a ride. I don't flatter myself that she's interested in my life. She wants to measure her experience of exile against mine, to see if it holds up. It doesn't. I can tell her that straight off.

Re: Coffee
9/2/2010 2:53 PM
From: Ivan Pyefinch
To: mia hakim

Hi mia,
It would be nice to meet you in person. As for driving by the house, it's quite a long way from where I live now. Let's see if there's time once you arrive. I look forward to your next section of the film.
Ivan

So much deflection, in all directions. I won't come out to say No about visiting the house. But more than that, I don't reveal my growing hunger for her script, or whatever it is she's sending me. Her words have the feel of a diary that transports me from the mundane world of driving tests. I feel privileged to help bring it into the world, and it whets my appetite to create something truly of my own.

"Can you get your nose out of your phone and help me over here," says Horace. "Have you seen the driver's book?"

17

WHATEVER MISGIVINGS Horace had yesterday have faded overnight. He pours his cereal with gusto, and sets Aida's pills in the eggcup without badgering her to take them. He has gathered his wallet and keys, and put them on the table in the foyer where he can find them.

"Today's the big day, Aida. I get my licence back."

"Won't that be nice."

Horace has skipped over some essential steps in the process, but I don't want to spoil his good mood. His confidence, as long as it doesn't extend to arrogance, may help him on the test.

Aida is moving slowly this morning, and there's no point in rushing her to get dressed. If he passes, Horace can have the extra pleasure of retelling Aida all about it at the cottage when we get home. If he fails, which is so much more likely, it may get ugly. Better that she's not an easy target for his rage.

There is a fall chill in the air as we approach Labour Day weekend, the symbolic end of summer vacation that falls like a portcullis. Every year, while Jerry Lewis prattled on the stage during his telethon, we would pack up the kitchen, the clothes, and the tools. Often it was wet or cool, and I would wear long pants for the first time in months. I was anxious to leave, anticipating the pleasure of rediscovering our house in Ottawa. Yet this pleasure was so short-lived and never measured up to expectation. The stale air in the house was stifling. I began to long for the cottage I had been so eager to leave only two hours before. I came to understand that I preferred to be in constant movement, to be neither here nor there. I tried to explain this once, linking it to Karen's belief that "life is a journey, not a destination", but it never washed. For her it just fed into my Nowhere Man persona.

Horace and I are halfway to Smiths Falls when I remember Aida's pills in the eggcup. She wasn't ready to eat before we left, and then I got distracted with the emails. When I leave for Ottawa, we will go back to Plan A: I get Aida on the phone, while Horace brings water and pills, and I encourage her to take them as we're talking. Otherwise Horace gets too frustrated with her or forgets altogether. I can understand. I have put the pills into her hand only to watch her put them down absently. Do they do any good? I have to believe her memory would be worse without them.

Horace sits behind the wheel of the Roadmaster before we enter the hospital. He puts his hands at ten and two, making turning motions. Then he adjusts the mirror with the care of someone about to drive. I'm surprised he hasn't asked for the keys.

"I think you'll probably do the test in one of their special cars with the extra brake."

"I know that."

I feel the sharpness of his tone right down to my toes. Seeing his crestfallen face is worse. He was clearly all set to do the test in his car, and I popped his bubble. I hear Karen in my head: Stop trying to protect him. It never works. He ends up blaming you.

The occupational therapist is waiting for us at the main entrance with a car and a clipboard. In her sensible pantsuit, she seems all business today, which removes the last scrap of hope left. The worst of all is this: I don't know if I want him to pass the test. It would certainly make our lives easier—his and mine. It's everyone else on the road who might suffer.

She opens the driver door, and I slide the seat back for him. I glance at the floor-mounted shift, and I know what's coming. This time, though, I keep my mouth shut.

With his stiff back, his head bumps against the top of the door frame, and he has to readjust his trajectory. I imagine Horace squeezing into the Harvard Trainer in 1944 in Scotland, sitting behind his student in the instructor's position. How limber he was then. If he hadn't bragged about his great piloting skills with the geriatric team, the psychiatrist might not have put so much stock in his failed clock test. That letter to the Ministry of Transport might never have happened. Instead, here we are, in freefall.

After his two failed attempts to slide into the seat, I cradle his head with one hand and guide his body in with the other. I'm like a cop helping a handcuffed man into the back of a police car. I squat down to his eye level, watching as he puts his right hand tentatively on the shift.

"It does the same thing," I tell him. "Once you get going, you won't have to shift at all. The car will practically drive itself."

My words are no comfort. He looks at me helplessly. If I could do the test for him, I would.

"We can't use my car? I'm more used to it."

"No. There's really no difference, Mr. Pyefinch. Any time you're ready."

She straightens the clipboard on her lap and stares out the windshield. At least it's not raining so he doesn't need to find the wipers.

"You'll be fine, Horace," I tell him. "Do your best. That's all you can do."

"That's right."

He manages a tiny smile, which nearly breaks my heart.

"Don't forget your seatbelt and to adjust your mirror," I tell him.

"Right."

As he straps himself in, with difficulty, the woman glares at me, shakes her head, and then ticks off a box on her chart. I lean over to kiss him, whispering "Your mirror" in his ear. He makes a big show of adjusting the position, then winks at me. This is Horace at his best.

On my mental checklist, I tick off all the conditions in his favour: no rain, but not too much sun either; small town traffic in mid-morning; the position of the car in front of the hospital, which means Horace doesn't have to back out of a parking spot, at least not right away. I start to hope he can actually pass this test. He drives slowly, and I can see him checking both ways two or three times before hitting the road. And then they disappear from view.

I sit on one of the vacant benches outside the front entrance, not far from an elderly man in a wheelchair hooked up to an IV. With each inhale of his cigarette, he hacks and spits. He glares, defying me to ask him to move the requisite ten feet from the entrance. I think of all the possible arcane rules of the road the therapist might throw at Horace, and my hopes for him fade again. In the 1970s, we watched *This is the Law,* a TV show of short vignettes where panellists tried to guess what obscure law was being broken. We could never guess the correct answer. But whereas I felt indifferent or, at worst, inadequate, Horace got enraged at the seeming injustice whenever he wasn't right. I often think that's the essential difference between us.

When they return, they sit in the No Stopping zone where she is either tallying his score or he is bargaining for another chance. I flash back to a Saturday trip to his office in downtown Ottawa. He had not wanted to waste a nickel so he gave it to me for the meter if I saw the "Green Hornets" coming. I gathered these were the people who checked for expired meters, but I had no idea what I was looking for. I shoulder checked constantly, surveying each pedestrian as a possible threat. When he returned, I pried open my palm, proudly handing him back the nickel. It took a few minutes to shake the cramp out of my fingers and for the impression of the coin to disappear from my skin. Maybe that's what inspired the idea for the tattoo on my wrist years later.

Horace opens his door fully, as if he's kicked at it in a fury. He stumbles forward, banging his head against the door frame again. He shakes off my attempts to help him.

"Goddamned government. Where the hell is my car?"

"It's right there in the first row. Do you see it? It's unlocked."

"In this place? They'll rob you blind."

I watch him thread his way through the parking lot without shoulder checking. His walk is determined, but wobbly all the same. Someone honks, and he raises his fist.

"Pedestrians have the goddamned right of way!"

Only after he has reached the passenger door safely and thrown himself into the Roadmaster do I turn to the occupational therapist. I bite back my first impulse, which is to apologize for his behaviour.

"He's clearly upset about failing the test," I say."

"He passed, actually."

She looks bemused, enjoying the sight of me standing with my mouth open waiting for words that won't come.

"Yes, my only real concern was that he was driving too cautiously."

Words are slowly forming in my brain and working their

way down to my mouth.

"Didn't you tell him he passed?"

"Of course."

"So why is he so upset?"

She pauses, relishing the dramatic moment.

"He wants to drive home today, and I told him it could take a few weeks for his licence to be reinstated. I'll start the paperwork before I leave today, but I can't promise it will be quick."

"I see."

"Good luck, then."

With this, she adjusts the front seat to fit her short legs, slips inside, and drives off. Horace is still stewing when I reach our car, although I pretend not to notice.

"Congratulations! You did it."

"Let's stop at the driver place when we pass through Brockville. I know the guy there."

"You think he'll get you the licence back faster, is that it?"

Surely, the occupational therapist will send her report in the next few minutes to Toronto. An agent at the ministry eager to clear the in-basket before the long weekend will adjust Horace's file immediately. When the fellow in the Brockville office looks up the file, he will see the amendment and, as a favour to Horace, print out a temporary licence.

I know enough not to challenge his magical thinking. Yet doesn't it happen almost exactly that way. I'm left standing at the counter, once again slack jawed. For Horace, it's the least they can do for taking his licence away. The only detail I have not foreseen is a new photo. It takes a few tries to get a neutral expression because Horace is scowling.

Out of habit he starts for the passenger side before grinning at his mistake. I put the keys in his hand without ceremony but not without trepidation. It's all too soon, too fast. Two days ago he was nearly crashing into a transport. He hasn't entirely forgotten the experience because he takes the river highway back to the cottage. I wonder how long before the old Horace returns.

Aida is leafing through a ten-year-old *Time* magazine when Horace returns triumphantly. Her nonchalant response to his victory sets him off, and he tells her she's wasting time reading old news. He disappears into the garage, his head full of plans to build a portable flag stand for the Remembrance Day parade two months from now.

By the evening we're all together again to watch the opening of the Jerry Lewis telethon. The show stays on throughout the weekend, just as it did in my childhood, except now I'm the only one packing up for Ottawa. Horace wants me at the train station early so he doesn't have to drive at night. I am relieved at his newfound defensive driving skills, even as I anticipate having too much time to feel queasy about leaving them on their own. At the same time I'm antsy for my freedom, just as Horace is anxious to see my back. By the time Jerry sings his traditional finale—"You Never Walk Alone"— Horace is pushing me out the door. I kiss Aida, who is teary-eyed either by the thought of my departure or, more likely, by the sight of Jerry choking up with emotion in the middle of his song.

On a holiday Monday, there's only one other person at the train station in Brockville, a young woman enveloped in a Toronto Maple Leafs' sweater. Her face seems to have been burned at some point, or perhaps it's a birthmark. With the announcement for the next train, she leaves the waiting room to wave at the engineer, who waves back. She has no bags with her, and I realize she's just passing the time.

"You're waiting for the Toronto train?" she asks.

"Ottawa."

"That's two hours' away."

I can't tell if she's pleased to show off her knowledge or happy for my company. She makes no more effort at conversation and neither do I, but each time a train arrives she nods before standing up. I don't know how she stands the noise on the platform. It seems such a high price to pay for a moment of connection.

When my train approaches, she shows me where to stand on the platform, and then keeps walking down the line. I wonder if she comes here every night and how long she stays. I can see her through the window standing under a light, but our car is already in darkness, and she doesn't see me wave goodbye.

FALL 2010

18

KAREN IS POKING her nose around my condo like she wants to buy it. At less than six hundred square feet, it's most certainly smaller than her apartment in Sandy Hill. But I own it, which makes it a curiosity, and it's in upscale Wellington West rather than in the university ghetto. We had only ever rented together, even after twenty years as a couple. Buying this place was me getting sucked into the vortex of the condo lifestyle ads, but I don't suggest it was anything but a deliberate and calculated decision.

"What happened to your chair?" she asks.

"In the shop. I sit on the ball. Better for the abs."

"They have a shop for chairs now?"

If she's expecting me to keep up the repartee, I'm disappointing her. I'm not exactly tongue-tied, but having agreed to meet for coffee, and then actually starting to look forward to it, I am deflated. Once again expectation outshines experience.

Now that Horace has the car again I'm not sure how to get that monster chair back to Ottawa unless I rent an SUV. This is not something Karen needs to know.

"A corner view of Epicurean Row," she says. "Nicely appointed."

Her mocking tone is a feint to disguise her true intent: a quick survey of the photos and postcards that I display under the heavy plate of glass on my desk. I filed them all away in June—the photos of us posed and impromptu that each evoked enough memories and feelings to fill a French-English dictionary twice over. Most came out easily, while others I had to pry off the underside of the glass with a letter opener. In that sense, my act was deliberate, but it was not part of a grand plan to get on with my life. I simply awoke one morning and felt it was right to do. The bathroom is likely her next stop. If I had been clever, I would have stuck a second toothbrush in the holder to suggest I had regular company. No, she moves next to the galley kitchen, where I've left open a cupboard door. Karen puts her hands on the handle as if to close it, then stops, out of respect or to avoid falling into old patterns. I often left drawers and cupboard doors open that she would then feel compelled to close. Our first therapist suggested I believed I could always come back later to close them, which meant I was holding on to the past. Our last one thought I was unconsciously wanting to be mothered. Maybe he's just lazy? Karen had suggested.

"What's all this, then?" she says, knocking on the pocket doors.

Her voice is faux innocent, an echo of an English bobby who's stumbled upon something racy. It's something one of us would say if we came upon the other dressing in the bedroom. On impulse, suddenly protective of my celibate life, I had pulled the doors shut while she was riding the elevator up to the fifth floor. I would like her to think I've got bras and panties from my various conquests hanging from the fake vintage bed frame. A dishevelled bed, at least, to suggest the occasional presence of a playmate instead of the dust bunnies.

"Can I have a quick pee before we go downstairs?" she says.

"Down the corridor, hang a right. You can't miss it."

She plays along, pretending to be puzzled, as if she needs GPS to find the one room in this place with a real door.

A skinny rectangular window above my bed lets light

from outside stream into the bathroom. I've often thought it has creepy *Psycho*-like potential, although I've so far had no occasion to be tempted. If Karen were taking a shower, would I look? I don't think so. Not out of respect, but rather out of fear of boredom. What's all this, then? We really didn't need to ask.

IT'S a fine fall afternoon so we sit at an outside table at the Bridgehead café with our coffees and banana bread. A greyish couple—both senior government managers, I'm guessing— eye her curiously over the tops of their weekend newspapers. A couple pushing a stroller laden with bags of fresh vegetables from the Parkdale Market just happen to untangle the leash of their Golden Retriever in front of our table. But they are only seeing her in one dimension. I'm mesmerized because I know what she once was.

Gone are the Patagonia fleece and cotton sweatpants from Mountain Equipment Co-op that she would typically wear on a weekend in autumn. Instead, she wears baggy turquoise pants and a sleeveless V-necked top in a shade of papaya topped up by a black kimono jacket. A shoulder bag has replaced the knapsack. Her brown page-girl hair has been grown out until it sits in jagged, yet precise, layers upon her shoulders.

I haven't been counting the days, but I know it's been two years since she moved out. My head is full of the usual clichés of estranged couples in such situations so I hold my tongue. After all, she texted me for this appointment.

"How are Horace and Aida?"

Is she humouring me, making fun, or genuinely interested? I can't read her face the way I once could.

"Still doing their thing."

"Glad to hear it."

She smiles then, tentatively. I remember the look from the lecture hall of first-year translation when we found each other again after high school. It says, "Yes, it's me. Can you believe we're here?" We both lived at home that first year, taking the same bus downtown from the west end for many of the same classes. By second year, after my parents retired and moved to the country, Karen and I had an apartment in a heritage mansion on Wilbrod, close to the university. Then we had a series of places in the Golden Triangle and the Glebe as we established our careers, ending with the bottom half of a house in Old Ottawa South. Still renters, yes, but we were getting ready to buy. Maybe it was the prospect of all that security that turned her the other way, back toward the student ghetto life we had left behind and the young guy to go with it.

"How are things with P'tit-Luc?"

I aim for an ironic tone, but it comes out with spittle. Some leftover resentment. Still.

"Bigger and better."

Out of fatigue, lack of interest, or compassion, she is letting me off easy. I would have preferred a groin kick. It would show she still cared.

"You're still wearing your ring," she says.

Her voice sounds anguished on my behalf. Like the decision to remove the photos, taking off the ring is not something to force. I don't feel compelled to explain, defend, apologize, or reassure. That's new for me.

"You've got to move on," she says.

She draws an impatient breath as she mistakes my silence for withdrawal. Again, I don't feel compelled to change her opinion of me. This feels new, too.

"You haven't changed, Ivan. You can't stay stuck like this."

It's my turn to draw in a tight breath, but again, I don't engage her. I'm tired, suddenly, and wondering what we're doing here.

"I wanted to see you this weekend to say goodbye, for real," she says.

Karen pulls at one of her own rings, probably a gift from Luc. It looks like a prize from a gum machine.

"We moved to Montreal. In July. There's no jazz scene here. We need more places to play, and people to play with. There's a real community…"

"You don't need to explain."

"You don't care that I've left? I didn't have to come here today. I've got a million things to do."

Karen pushes her chair back from the table, a gesture usually followed by me backtracking on whatever I've said, convinced that a retraction can right the wrong. An old feeling rises up inside—a desire, almost paternal, to take care of her. It typically precedes a dose of resentment at her unconscious expectations, and my need to make her grateful for having saved her. This endless cycle of recrimination and reconciliation wore us out.

"You don't want your banana bread?" I ask. "There are children starving in China."

It's something both our fathers would say at the dinner table. My nod to our shared past is enough to make her laugh. She makes a show of pulling in her chair again. For once, I've managed a manoeuvre that preserves both of our dignities.

She launches into her own promotional pamphlet for her neighbourhood in Montreal with its mix of anglos and francos, Hassidic Jews, bagel shops, *friperies* and clubs. If the music thing doesn't work out, she could always try real estate. It's annoying, how she's already saying they're renting a "five-and-a-half" rather than a "two-bedroom." But part of me is envious at how she is reinventing herself. She has thrown away her marriage, her career, and her home for the sake of love, art, and self-renewal. Meanwhile, I burrow into debt on Epicurean Row, feeding off the scraps of fewer and fewer contracts, taking care of my parents whether they want me to or not. I fight the impulse to tell Karen about Mia's translation. She will think I'm trying to compete, and she'll be right. More than that I want to keep the work private. As a woman, Karen would have been the better choice of translator right from the start. Now that she's left for Montreal, Karen has the sensibility of an exile as well. I play with the arm of my coffee mug. Horace would often make fun of how I gripped my glass of milk at meals as if afraid someone would take it.

"So how are you doing?" she says. "Lots of work?"

"Slow and steady wins the race."

"Sailing metaphors, how I've missed them. If you're living here, I guess you're doing all right."

Let her think that one aspect of my life is not an unmitigated failure. Our coffees finished, we each push down on the crumbs of banana bread on our plates so they adhere to our fingertips. We don't lick them off each other's fingers, but from our shared glance we acknowledge that we once did. We're not unique. I'm sure, early on at least, even Horace and Aida shared a private language that brought them closer together. But when I think of Horace at the age I am now, he seemed so grown up. Karen and I, deep down, are still nine-year-olds spinning the bottle. Maybe if we'd had a child of our own we would have shed our baby fat.

"It's your birthday next week," I say.

My words aren't planned and I regret them immediately. They sound like an overture to hang on.

"I should really get going," she says.

I get up from the table at the same time. Purely for optics. I don't want to be left behind one more time. Will we hug, air-kiss on each cheek, or French kiss again by accident?

"Can I use your bathroom again?"

Karen has saved us from a potentially awkward departure on the sidewalk. Yet having her in my place again feels intrusive.

We ride the elevator in silence. Are we so intimate there is no need for words? Or are we two strangers anxious for an uncomfortable moment to pass? Both and neither. I tug at my ring.

While I unlock my door, I think of all the times coming home together with Karen. She would rush ahead, anxious to pee, fumbling in her knapsack for keys until, fed up, I reached into my pockets and opened the door for her. Even if she carries a shoulder bag now, I'm sure that part of her life hasn't changed.

She closes the bathroom door, but doesn't lock it, not like earlier. She feels more at home now maybe. Next she'll spread open the pocket doors. As I think the words, part of me wants it to happen, and wonders if she does, too. Not that we were ever lovers prone to spontaneity. Sex could be passionate, but it was deliberate.

"Thanks. My teeth were swimming."

She smiles brightly, looking around my place again. Instead of moving toward the front door, she heads toward the balcony. She slides the door open, steps out to the railing, and points to the café below. I stand beside her.

"Someone's already taken our table," she says.

"It had to happen."

"But so soon?"

Her voice is shaking, and she pulls me in tight for a hug. Her tears are wet on my cheek. I feel the weight of her body against mine, suspended in mid-air by reinforced asphalt underfoot.

"You'll be okay," I tell her.

She laughs, bitterly it seems to me. This was not how it was supposed to go, me reassuring her. By mutual agreement we don't kiss. We are beyond that now.

"If you're ever stuck with too much work, I'll be happy to help you out," she says.

"Everyone's just getting back to the office after summer vacation. You know how it goes. But, sure, if I have too much, I'll let you know."

"I mean it. Like we used to help each other out. That would be okay, right?"

"No worries."

"Would it be too much to ask for an advance? We've got so many expenses. With the move and settling in."

I turn my head so she doesn't see the disappointment in my face. Her voice strains so hard to sound casual and spontaneous. But all this, I realize, was planned from the start. Maybe not the tears, but everything else. It cheapens the time we've just had together. Yet in the manipulation is an assumed intimacy. The Ivan she knows would never refuse or hurt her. I might resent her after the fact, but she'll be long gone. Even so, I know this is difficult for her, with either a Yes or a No bringing its own set of humiliations. She has not considered that I might have changed.

With my back to her, I open a drawer in my desk for my cheque book, and write one out for more than I can afford, but probably less than she needs. In another life, I might have handed it over with a flourish, holding it from the edges and forcing her to receive it in her palm and read the amount. This time, I fold the cheque in half, and she takes it between her thumb and forefinger, placing it in her bag without looking. Our eyes meet again, both of us knowing this is not a retainer for future services or even a loan. She brings me tight again and whispers "Thank you" into my ear, her lips lightly touching my neck. Then she is gone. As I close my desk drawer, I take off the ring and place it in the tray beside the paper clips—*les trombones*.

19

TWO WEEKS WITHOUT my chair is long enough. I pick up the SUV rental first thing Friday morning, and then leave it in the underground parking of the condo all day to get my money's worth out of the spot. It's the kind of logic Horace would appreciate, but that would infuriate Karen, if only she knew. It's liberating to realize she doesn't.

I skip the drive past my childhood home in the west end, saving up my nostalgia for Mia's visit in November. I've come around to sharing this part of my past with her. But we will meet for coffee somewhere besides the Bridgehead downstairs. Some places have too much history.

THE road committee, in its wisdom, put off paving the cottage road until the spring. It makes no sense to me, but I don't ask questions. The cycle of the seasons is change enough for Horace. The ferns have already died off, giving me a clear view of the Roadmaster parked in front of the white garage. I swing onto the main lawn, and park under the pine trees. The needles are only starting to turn, and the same goes for the oak and maple leaves. Horace might be ready to pack it all in for the fall, but the trees have their own ideas. They must have soaked up some of his independent streak when he planted them sixty years ago. Last year the leaves fell so late we gathered them up in spring, me raking onto the tarp and Horace blowing the rest over the cliff. We picked a nice day in May for it, but underneath the brittle leaves on top were clumps still heavy with moisture and earth. Horace had a hard time blowing them out. He had to jam the machine right into the pile to stir them up. Many resisted.

He has set up his work bench on the stone patio outside the blue garage to give himself elbow room. Despite his best efforts, the garage is overrun with tools—the industrial-sized lathe in the corner with which he turned out six-foot standing lamps, the smaller lathe that he has never used, the band saw and table saw, the jointer, and the drill press. Plus all the small hand tools perched on any available surface, and odds and ends like a deflated basketball. On a shelf he has stretched across the width of the garage are baby food jars full of finishing nails and screws side-by-each with orange juice containers full of nuts and bolts. It's high enough that he won't bang his head against it, but it gets in the way of the garage door. Although it only rises two-thirds of the way up, friction from the stiff hinges keeps it in place. Horace ducks each time he goes into the garage. A small price to pay, really.

The basketball hoop, rusted now and net-less, extends out from the garage high above his head like a halo. He was the star captain of the high school basketball team, and wanted me to experience the same glory. In the championship photo from 1938 that hangs in the foyer of the cottage, Horace—his smile self-assured, his hair gelled into a tidal wave—stands a full foot higher than his scrawny friend Bob. The coach played Horace until he could hardly stand. Did Bob play at all? Horace taught me a few shots, which my gym teacher assured me hadn't been used since the 1950s. I never told Horace, protecting the memories of his glory years and his dreams for me. I stood on the edge of the road, spinning the ball from my waist rather than attempting a lay-up. If I missed, the ball would often bounce against a boulder and then hit the blue aluminum door with a thundering crash, as if Zeus himself were expressing his displeasure from the heavens.

Horace has built a square box out of thick plywood to serve as a mobile flag stand for the Remembrance Day service. He wants to carry the flag during the march from City Hall to the Cenotaph, and then plant it in the stand at the foot of the statue behind the dignitaries and wreaths. It seems unlikely they'll allow his homemade flag and box anywhere near the pomp and ceremony, but I could be wrong.

With his back to me, and focused on drilling a hole in the top of the box, Horace doesn't see or hear me drive through the two pillars onto the main lawn. Aida, though, is standing on the front patio in her pink sweater with arms crossed, as if she is expecting me. Maybe she is. I sometimes think she has an extra sense. I once fell out of a tree in the woods far from the cottage, too far for her to have heard my gasps for breath. Yet there she was.

"There you are," Aida says.

She hugs me with the affection of a little girl for her father. I take care not to press too deeply into her bony back.

Even if Horace managed to prepare fresh food, I suspect she wouldn't eat enough to restore her vitality. I follow her back into the cottage and allow her to make me tea. The throw carpets that I threw into the garage have magically reappeared in front of the sink, perfectly placed for either of them to trip over. I will need to take more drastic action, hauling them out after dark and hiding them in my car so I can take them away safely, this ticking time bomb.

She pours water into two mugs, and heats them in the microwave. I set out a few cookies. A real tea party, and why not? No one comes to visit anymore or invites her out. In truth, our extended family began to distance itself from Horace first, beginning in the mid-1990s when he became obsessed with the death of his friend Bob after my tattoo.

Horace bursts into the room while we're sipping our tea.

"Have a cookie, dear," Aida says.

He pulls up a chair, grinning, shaking his head, and reaches for a dark chocolate Celebration biscuit before launching into his story. So often it was like this in my childhood— my conversations with Aida stopped in mid-flight when Horace entered the room. But there is no collusion with Aida anymore, no more rolling our eyes together secretly laughing at how Horace was oblivious to others. It was always only a survival tactic, a way to keep our head above water around him, to pretend we were superior. The first ten years were the hardest because I wanted more attention from him. But then, once my body became acclimatized to his indifference, I no longer felt the sting. I simply let my mind drift until he finished, letting his words spark my own reveries.

"...got the damned pipe to fit the hole..."

Launching my sailboat, with Horace on the stone dock watching as I waded knee-high in water with the mast, the single sail flapping and snapping around me, lifting it high enough to get the leverage needed to slip the mast into the hole, the water gushing out from the pressure, the exhilaration of hearing Horace cheering me on

"…not stable, it could tip over any moment…"

Catching the mainsheet on the edge of the stern, locking the boom and sending the boat over, me clutching the gunwale

"…the solution's right in front of me…"

Flipping my legs over to stand on the centreboard, rocking and squatting to raise it up, the shower of water from the sail as I got back in the cockpit and freed the boom, that exquisite sensation of liberation as the boat shot off.

"…stones from the river."

Hauling stones up the fire escape on a dolly with help from the neighbours, Horace on the middle landing to guide the dolly up on the plywood he had set down on the metal rungs, Aida behind the wheel of the Country Squire ready to haul up the contraption with the rope attached to the trailer hitch, me at the top of the stairs, ever the go-between, ready to give Aida the signal and make sure the rope didn't catch.

As Horace finishes his story, I bring my own memories into the present.

"Do you remember hauling up stones to build the patio?" I ask him.

Horace looks at me, his forehead wrinkled in concentration, but he can't retrieve this forty-year-old memory.

"You got the neighbours to help. It took four men to lift some of those stones."

He grins, but his face still looks blank. He is reliving the moment through me.

"It's a long way up from the river carrying rocks for your flag stand," I tell him. "Maybe we can find some bricks in the back forty."

"Now you're thinking. I'll have a look right now."

With a whirl of his torso, he is gone again. A few moments later Aida has forgotten he was even there, while I am still catching my breath from the intensity of his presence. It doesn't take as long to breathe normally as it once did. That's something, at least. The big difference between then and now, the one that gnaws at me, is that I'm swimming here alone. The current has taken Aida out of reach.

Outside the garage, Horace has already filled the box with bricks, and is securing the lid again.

"That's not going anywhere now," he says. "The wind can blow the flag all it wants."

Sure enough I tap the box with my foot and it doesn't move. How we're going to move this around easily on Remembrance Day is a question I don't broach.

"Put it in," he says. "You'll see how it fits."

I grab the pole with the stiff flag atop and manoeuvre it above the pipe that sticks out of the lid. I approach from the roadside so I don't get tangled up with the basketball hoop. Unlike the hole for the mast in my sailboat, the pipe is narrow and unforgiving—more like the size of a flag marking the hole on a golf course. The weight of the flag also throws off my balance and I circle around the pipe a few times before getting it to fit. I wonder what those marines felt planting the American flag at Iwo Jima—elation, pride, or simply, like me, relief?

Often Horace gets deflated after a project is finished. He doesn't like the feeling of not knowing what to do next. But today he keeps bustling, first pulling the flag out of the pipe and then bending down to lift the box.

"Wait," I tell him. "You'll hurt your back."

Even with two of us, it's a struggle to get the box onto the Workmate. I imagine us on Remembrance Day, the fibres of the plywood brushing onto Horace's uniform as we transfer it from the Roadmaster to the Cenotaph. Maybe we should carry the bricks separately, and pile them in once the box is in place.

"It just needs some paint," he says. "You coming?"

"You don't have any good paint in here?"

I point to the shelves along the east wall of the garage lined with paint cans. Most in litres, probably, but some going back to gallons.

"Christ, no. That's all garbage."

I don't ask why he doesn't throw them out. Instead, I follow him back to the cottage, suggesting Aida might come with us to town.

"She's happy enough here," he says.

"She needs to get out more."

"Well, you look after her then."

But Aida is heading to bed for a nap. I'm torn over who needs more looking after, even as I realize I'm only here for the weekend. Thinking I can save one or both of them from danger—Karen calls this playing my Angel card. It's totally fitting, she says, that the son of the Creator's Miracle Man has a messiah complex. While I'm musing, Horace plucks the photo of him and Bob in their cadet uniforms, circa 1941, from the wall in the foyer. That small action pushes me over the edge toward Horace. Somehow the idea of him wandering the aisles of the hardware store telling war stories makes me nervous. In case Aida gets up for tea, I bring the throw carpet with me. Thankfully she never thinks to use the stove.

"What are you doing with that?" Horace asks.

It's garbage, I want to say. Like your paint.

"It's dangerous," I tell him. "You or Aida could slip on it really easily."

"The floor in the kitchen is damn cold."

"Then buy slippers."

"What am I, five years old?"

"You need to start thinking about how to prevent falls," I tell him. "It's like defensive driving, right? Taking a little extra time is better than having an accident."

As I say these words, I'm holding the steering wheel for him. Since I've been old enough to sit beside him in the car, he has left me to hold the wheel while he attaches his seatbelt. I'm not sure which is more incredible: his expectation that I will do it without him asking or that I actually do it. Once again, I'm left wondering how he manages without me. Somehow he must. One day I will not take the wheel and see where we land.

The downtown hardware store in Brockville is human-sized, not like the cavernous Home Depot, and the owner has known Horace for years. We're in and out in ten minutes with a half-litre of white.

"I need a Xerox across the street," he says.

It's hard to follow Horace's thoughts, harder still to predict them. There is a connection between the photocopy and the paint. It takes a few minutes before it comes to me.

"You want to put that photo of you and Bob on the flag stand."

"Once it's all white, you'll be able to see it better."

He's moving fast with his purposeful stride when his foot catches on the rubber runner inside the copy shop. He stumbles forward, dropping the framed photo but recovering his balance by grasping the counter. The clerk is a non-descript man in his forties, the kind I see everywhere in Riverton and Brockville. Thinning hair, a little paunch, glasses. He's probably been in this town his whole life, stuck in a minimum wage job with nowhere to go. He starts with alarm at Horace's arrival, and rushes around the counter. The two of us have got paws on Horace from either side, but he shakes us off. He's more concerned with the photo. It's not broken, having landed on the rubber mat. I hand it to him and he grins.

"Another miracle," he says.

"That was quite a spill you had, sir. Are you alright?"

"That was nothing."

Horace launches into his story about the uncontrollable spin in the Harvard, falling from ten thousand feet and then recovering just before the plane hit the ground.

"This photo, this photo," he says, unable to finish.

He looks to me helplessly.

"This is a photo of my father and his best friend Bob when they were cadets. Bob was the first man to volunteer from Brockville, and the first to die. A training accident. He wanted to be a pilot, and my father here was determined to fulfill his dream. So he signed up. He was so afraid of failure that he worked non-stop, and graduated at the top of his class. They made him an instructor in Scotland. That story he just told you, about the bad spin, what makes it even more special ..."

"I had this photo with me in the plane. Bob was the angel on my shoulder. I'm the Creator's Miracle Man, and he did it again just now. I could have cracked my skull. Bob was there."

The clerk nods, squeezing Horace's arm.

"This a real special photo and we'll take good care of it for you. What would you like?"

It takes three or four tries before Horace is satisfied with the size and shading. We're the only customers so the clerk doesn't seem to mind, or else he feels guilty for the bunched-up rubber mat. He probably thinks we'll tell the boss what happened. I'm tempted.

"You've got a good spot for the 11th of November," Horace tells him. "Keep your eyes peeled. I'll be walking by with my flag."

"Well, the store will be closed, but I'll be in the crowd looking for you."

The clerk waves off the charge for the copies. Horace beams. One more miracle thanks to Bob.

"You won't get in trouble with the boss?" Horace asks with a grin.

The clerk grins back.

"Not likely. I own the store."

Horace sticks out his hand. He has a thing for authority figures. I have a thing for reading people wrong.

With the Cenotaph not far away, Horace wants to do some reconnaissance. Glancing up the street toward City Hall, I can't picture Horace carrying his flag for the length of the parade, even in his wool uniform. Last year it was spitting snow at the veterans.

Beneath the statue, Horace paces around as if looking for the perfect spot to bury treasure.

"Have you talked to the organizers about your plans?" I ask.

"The head guy knows all about it."

"They'll have microphones up here, plus all the wreaths and other flags."

Horace is too focused on the photocopied picture to hear me. He's holding it up, imagining how it will look on his box.

Once back to the car, he hands me the keys and dozes

off beside me, the framed photo in his lap. Although I expect him to wake up as we pass the cemetery where Bob is buried, he sleeps right through. It's only the gravel road of the cottage that stirs him. When he's dozy, Horace can be more open to suggestion so I decide to reinforce my main message of the day.

"I was thinking we should get someone to help with Aida," I tell him. "She needs more mental stimulation, and someone to watch over her. You're busy with your projects. You can't always be there."

"We'll be back at the house soon."

"She's in danger there, too."

"What is all this danger you're talking about?"

"You said yourself that you could have cracked your skull today."

"Bob was looking out for me."

I don't have an answer for that. Aida is up when we get back, happy to see us.

She is favouring her leg again.

20

I see myself as akin to a painter before a blank canvas. She has mixed her pigments with science and care. In the back of her mind, she has years of study and knowledge of the history of art. But she does not plan to paint a portrait or even a landscape. She has entered the world of her childhood. She gets up early. She sets up the easel on the balcony. She lets herself be overtaken by the blue and gold hues around her. She prepares to paint her canvas, all with the same fear, excitement, and freedom as her first painting. Except now she has experience. It guides her choices. The emotion of return stirs her memory.

I want to explore my film with a map but also with stories from the past. The journey itself is the treasure. So the film will contain images and words from my point of view. A very personal film, yet I will not appear on the screen. But the viewer hears me think, reflect, compare, and feel. An intimate film, yes, but one that speaks about, and to, those who live elsewhere than the country where they were born.

Sex change
9/25/2010 3:25 PM
From: mia hakim
To: Ivan Pyefinch
Dear Ivan,

Something is missing in the last translation, as if I write with my heart and you translate with your head. I like my sentences to be waves that go on (and on), because they must be like my films, too much to contain in one breath, lava rolling from a volcanic eruption that takes everything in its path. I sense you removing all the rough edges and imperfections, which, to me, are the essence of how I approach cinema, the forces that bring it to life. My sentences need to breathe more, they are shaped to death. I'm sorry but it reads like an instruction manual. "She does this" and then "she does that". I find it bizarre that you have made the painter a woman out of some very Canadian sense of being proper. I know, as does everyone else, that I am a woman, and you know very well "painter" is masculine so you don't need to perform a sex change operation in the English. This is so different from everything you've done, I ask what has changed for you. Are you working in the same way as before? I picture you at your desk in Ottawa, at your computer. Am I wrong?

Amitiés,
mia

Re: Sex Change
9/25/2010 3:43 PM
From: Ivan Pyefinch
To: mia hakim
Dear mia,

I am at my desk in Ottawa, yes, but you are right — something has changed. All the other translations of your text were done at a cottage in the countryside, where I have been staying in August. I don't know why it should be different here, because this is where I normally work. If anything, my work at the cottage should have been weaker because although I had my good chair I lacked a proper desk. But maybe because I did not really want to be there I was closer to the spirit of exile. I will try to make it better.

Re: Sex change
9/25/2010 3:51 PM
From: mia hakim
To: Ivan Pyefinch
Why did you not want to be there?

Re: Sex change
9/25/2010 3:57 PM
From: Ivan Pyefinch
To: mia hakim

The cottage has been in my family since the 1950s. It actually belongs to me now, on paper, as my father has signed over the ownership. I have my earliest memories there, but it is also associated with various types of disappointment. I want to go, but often end up regretting that it doesn't live up to my expectations. This time I went because my parents are not well. My father lost his driver's licence (he got it back) so I was playing chauffeur during August. My mother has Alzheimer's and so needs more help. They are still managing, but the time is coming when they won't be able to stay at the cottage, or anywhere else, on their own.

Re: Sex Change
9/25/2010 4:12 PM
From: mia hakim
To: Ivan Pyefinch

This must be a difficult situation, and I'm sorry that I have been imposing my translation on you all this time. If you want, we can stop.

Re: Sex change
9/25/2010 4:16 PM
From: Ivan Pyefinch
To: mia hakim
Doing your translation while I was at the cottage kept me sane. I would be sad if we stopped.

Re: Sex change
9/25/2010 4:22 PM
From: mia hakim
To: Ivan Pyefinch
Okay, we keep going! Maybe it was the raw feelings of being at the cottage that allowed you to get at something? You said before you didn't want to be there. Maybe it's because you are fearful of losing what little you have. I feel some of this when I think of going back to Tunisia. My grandfather owned four summer homes (!) They would be divided between his four sons and their families each year for our holidays. Everyone wanted the house on the beach, and my father always got the winning straw. The memories of those summers are the few from my childhood that have some joy, although my sister and I did not get along. I am afraid to go back. I'm afraid of being in touch with the pain. I'm afraid it will erase that goodness from my heart. Look at these short sentences. You are poisoning me!

Re: Sex change
9/25/2010 4:26 PM
From: Ivan Pyefinch
To: mia hakim
I will be going back to the cottage again soon to help my father close it up for the winter. If you have something else ready, I will work on it in my room there. Maybe we will see a difference.

Re: Sex change
9/25/2010 4:53 PM
From: mia hakim
To: Ivan Pyefinch
All those rats with tails running around getting ready for winter!

I don't know what's involved in this closing work, but it sounds like a sad time. And then there is your childhood home in Ottawa that you spoke about, which also stirs up melancholy. Is the cottage far? When I come to visit, can you go there after we drive past your house? It looks like I will be coming around November 10th.

Re: Sex change
9/25/2010 5:22 PM
From: Ivan Pyefinch
To: mia hakim
The cottage is about an hour from Ottawa. I actually need to be there for Remembrance Day, which is the 11th. He is a veteran from WW II, and it means a lot to him, especially this year. So a trip up to the cottage might not work very well. Let's play it by ear.

Re: Sex change
9/25/2010 6:11 PM
From: mia hakim
To: Ivan Pyefinch
I'm sorry, I'm intruding on your private life. It's not enough that I ask you to do this translation for me!

Re: Sex change
9/25/2010 6:29 PM
From: Ivan Pyefinch
To: mia hakim
It's not an intrusion. It's only that I need to focus on my parents on that day. My father wants to bring a homemade flag to the parade, and I'm anticipating a disaster.

Re: Sex change
9/25/2010 7:18 PM
From: mia hakim
To: Ivan Pyefinch
I hate flags! But would it help if I looked after your mother during the parade? It would be a small way to repay you... unless you have someone you're going with already to help.

Re: Sex change
9/25/2010 7:22 PM

From: Ivan Pyefinch
To: mia hakim
I was going on my own. Let's see how you feel when you get here. Do you have a place to stay in Ottawa? I have a couch.

IT takes me a few minutes before I hit Send. This woman is about to resume a relationship with an old lover in Tunisia, and I'm inviting her to stay with me. Would I really bring her to Riverton for the parade, the box of bricks, and the unflappable flag?

 21

WHEN I ARRIVE at the cottage, the Roadmaster is parked under the apple tree to give us space to work in front of the white garage. Horace is on the cliff, pulling the flag staff out of the hollow pipe in the ground. Any other nylon flag might be swishing in the breeze and getting in his face, but it's sewn on so tight that it doesn't even catch any wind. The metal frame, which weighs his creation to one side, throws him off balance. He teeters backward toward empty space, does a little two-step forward, then lets the staff crash down on the top railing of the fence and the flag itself tips over unharmed onto the grass. By the time I rush there from the car, he's grinning and waving at me. Whether he's saving face or blasé about another Bob-manufactured miracle, I'm not sure.

"You finally made it," he says.

"Right on time, in fact."

"Come on, then."

He picks up the flag, carrying it like a lance toward his station wagon.

"I've painted the flag box," he says. "Come have a look."

"Let me say hi to Aida first."

"We don't have all day."

"I'm staying overnight so, yeah, we do."

"Do what?"

"Have all day."

"I want to do the water first and get that done. Then get the shutters ready, and then pull up the dock."

"You don't want to do the dock first? We might need the bathroom this afternoon."

"Don't tell me what to do. I've done this a hundred times."

I'm thinking this is only the second autumn for his crazy dock but don't say it. It will only aggravate him more than me not seeing his flag box right away.

Aida is in her familiar spot, wrapped up in a couple of blankets. It's cooler in the cottage than out.

"You look cozy," I tell her.

"There's a chill in the air."

"You'll be moving back to the house in a few days. It'll be warmer there."

"We should be in Florida."

This might be a conscious lament for having sold their winter home or an unconscious echo of that experience radiating from some corner of her mind. Either way I don't know how to respond. I peck her on the cheek and fill up her tea.

"I'll be working with Horace outside for a while, and then we'll have lunch."

"You keep an eye on him. He's been mean to me."

"Really? What's he done?"

"Oh, he knows."

I haven't heard this tone in months. Maligned, knowing,

superior. All for a slight real or imagined, recent or old. Maybe it was a word or gesture that she would like to spit out, as if it went down the wrong way.

"I won't be too long," I tell her.

"You take your time, dear, and don't worry about me."

Horace is out near the road, opening the valve at the well head. That means he's already shut off the water in the pump house. In a hurry, as always. I move to the east side of the cottage to open the valve that connects to the garden hose.

"Stop! Whoa! Whoa!"

Horace rushes up to me, eyes wide, breath short. He waves his arms high in the air, deep-rooted fear overcoming the downward force of his rounded shoulders.

"Did you touch it?"

"I just got here."

He bends down to check, then needs my help to get up without falling forward.

"It's open now for sure," he says.

"I never touched it."

My voice has an edge now too. How quickly I fall into defensive posture, as if an inexplicable force is carrying me backward toward a childhood full of getting things wrong. Yet he's right. With the best of intentions, I might have closed it again. Any trapped water would have frozen this winter, bursting the pipe in the spring thaw. Would I have known if the valve were open or closed? I don't dispute my incompetence with all things mechanical, only the need for such panic.

Inside the cottage, we open the faucets in the kitchen and bathroom and I climb the stepladder with the trouble light, using my head to push up the ceiling board that leads to the attic. Once I can get a grip, I flip the board on its side, leaning it against the joists. I took over the job of opening and closing pipes last year. I insisted, saying I needed to learn, although I was more worried about him on the ladder. He had walked me through the process from below, his pristine instructions informed by having set up the system sixty years ago. I shine the light on the complex array of pipes, some leading to the hot water tank, others heading toward the bathroom and shower behind me, still others heading east toward the far end. I can't remember one word of what he said.

"Shut off the hot water," he says. "The box is to your right, sitting on the rafter. You can feel for it in the dark, you don't need to swing the light. It can only go one way, but you'll need two hands to pull the lever because it's stiff."

"And the valves on the pipes?" I ask. "There's a green one, a red one and …"

"Jesus, don't touch those. Hand me the hose that's connected to the bottom of the tank. Be careful."

Without looking, I know he's wrapping the floppy part of the hose in a towel sitting on the rack on the inside of the bathroom door. With the force of the hot water, the hose can easily slip and spurt water everywhere, and the towel keeps it secure. Then he'll stick the end of the hose down the bathroom sink. Ridiculous, but I feel a surge of pride that I've remembered that much.

"Now open the cut-off valve at the bottom of the tank. It's just above the hose. Be careful. It can break easily. Do you hear the water running?"

When I think of how he forgets things—where he left his wallet or the grocery list or all the once familiar words and names—his detailed recollection for the layout of the water system reassures me. Through sheer force of repetition it has been engrained in his mind, even if closing up only happens once a year. In the spring, he will tell me where to look for the green and red valves, and how to shut them off before we turn the water on again. Then we'll test each section of the pipes, one by one, for leaks. I've filmed it all on my Blackberry because I don't trust my memory for anything mechanical.

While the tank drains, we move out to the white garage to gather the shutters. With the canoe sitting on two horses in the middle, and two stacks of pine barn boards on either side, it's more jam-packed than the blue garage. The thirteen shutters lean against the stack of boards on the right, boards retrieved from an old barn being torn down. Decades ago, he fashioned some of the boards on his lathe into fancy standing lamps and perpetual calendars. All I can think is the time for woodworking projects has passed. One day, this garage will be falling down, and someone will stumble on this treasure trove of heritage wood and be happy.

The first few shutters are the easiest, but I have to stretch for the others because there's no space for my feet to move. Even then I have to wiggle the shutters because they grip on the sand floor. I do this job because Horace can't bend his body anymore in the tight space. With the canoe on the other side, there's no room to fall down, but it's easy to lose your footing. I teeter over twice myself, my body falling gently against the stack.

He is content to take each shutter and stack it against the edge of the garage. When they're all out, we pile them widthwise on the wheelbarrow and take them across the road to the cottage. Only three at a time because they're heavy. After the tops of the shutters rotted, he added a new piece of plywood that essentially doubled the thickness.

He insists on wheeling, while I walk alongside to make sure it doesn't tip over. The wheels of the barrow are soft, which throws off his balance. With the boards extending on either side like the wings of a plane, he looks like a pilot who is out of control. We lean the shutters against the apple tree until we're ready to hook them up.

We sit for a few minutes inside to catch our breath, and to listen for the last gasps of air in the hot water tank. I could happily take a longer break, but Horace is anxious to finish. I open the valve behind the shared wall separating the bathroom and my old bedroom. It sits awkwardly under the last shelf of a bookcase Horace installed when he built the new addition in 1983. Then it's on to the kitchen for the two valves under the sink and the dishwasher. Last year, the set screw in the dishwasher valve came loose while Horace was in the garage. Aida was in the kitchen, washing a few dishes by hand, having forgotten to stack them in the machine. She stood helplessly as the water rose to her ankles and poured through the open doorway onto the carpet in the dining room. In another late miracle, Horace came into the cottage for something, discovered the disaster, and ran outside to shut off the pump. They haven't used the dishwasher since, but he still needs to connect it in spring and disconnect it in the fall. I give him space to bend down and lie on his side, holding the light for him. As the last step, I drain the toilet and tank, spooning out and then sponging the last dregs of water. I stuff an orange pool noodle down the bowl to keep the smell from the septic tank from penetrating the cottage during the winter.

When we're finished, Horace allows himself to stumble with fatigue into the chair beside Aida.

"What do you think, Aid?" he says. "Almost done. We'll leave the shutters and the fridge for another day, but I want to haul up the dock."

"I need to use the bathroom," she says.

Aida pronounces the word "bawthroom" in a self-conscious imitation of an uppercrust Brit. Despite everything, her sense of irony is still intact. Sometimes.

"We just shut the water off," Horace says. "You'll need to go in the woods."

Aida laughs, but I hear satisfaction in Horace's tone, his anger at what she has become.

"Margaret lives here full-time now," I tell her. "I'm sure her toilet's working."

"Does she?" Aida says.

"She voted to pave the goddamned road," says Horace, to my surprise. Somehow word has filtered down to him or maybe he gleaned more from the road meeting than I thought.

I escort Aida to Margaret's place, walking past the shutters leaning against the tree. His mobile flag stand is sitting on the Workmate outside the main garage in all its freshly painted glory. He's already taped the photo of him and Bob on one side. There is no way the organizers will let him park that thing on the Cenotaph.

Aida takes my arm as if out for a Sunday stroll in the country with her beau. Her sleeve rides up slightly, and I see her wrist is black and blue.

"Does that hurt?" I ask her.

"Oh, a little. I must have banged it on something."

Either she fell or Horace grabbed her wrist in frustration. Neither bodes well. "You said before that Horace was mean to you."

"I didn't mean to."

There is no self-conscious chuckle at the word play. Her sentence comes out more like an apology. But for what? Slandering Horace's good name by suggesting he took out his anger on her? I think of all the women who say they've walked into doors rather than risk more abuse from their husbands. Or is Aida sorry that her mind is playing tricks, making her disremember?

Margaret is home, and happily takes in Aida while I finish up with Horace. I see him standing motionless on the edge of the cliff with a coil of high-strength steel in his hands. He teeters again and I start to run.

"It's all wrong," he says. "I've been pulling, but it's not the right one."

"It's hooked up to the fire escape on the first landing," I tell him. "We need to release it, and hook it up to the dock. You rigged up some kind of winch down there. This steel just holds the weight."

"Oh to hell with it, let's do it next time."

He bends to hook the coil carefully back on the stake in the cliff. As he turns, his foot catches against the hollow pipe he installed to hold his flag. He stumbles forward, and I grab his wrist to stop him tumbling over the edge, swinging him toward the cottage where his knees land on the grass. He stays still a moment, as if praying, and then rubs where I grabbed him.

22

I understand little of my childhood. I don't know how it was for others, but no one took the time to explain who I was and what I was doing there, in Tunisia. No one spoke to me about religion, tradition, heritage, mother tongue, culture, independence, or exile. I grew up with my questions. For example, the Arabic language, why did it disappear after primary school?

Mired in dread from an early age, I mixed up everything. The separation of my parents from the communities in Tunisia, Jewish and Muslim, the personal and the political. That I survived a life of silence and prohibitions I owe to the Arab women who selflessly hid my loneliness in the shadow they cast. For as long as I remember, in the city, close to the sea or the desert, there was a language between us that went beyond words. They never seemed to be alone, and I took refuge with them.

But I never had the chance, within all the unexpected moments of my childhood, to experience the mysteries of life and death that were transmitted through each gesture, each word, each step, of these women. They remained tucked away like a treasure at the bottom of a well.

I am often offended by the western view of Arab-Muslim women as "submissive victims." I don't see it in the faces of the Tunisian women of my early childhood, those who taught me pride and resistance, a sense of generosity and justice, and who were my sole source of protection, grace, and knowledge.

I SIT with the desert sand on my face, the salt from the sea on my tongue, the texture of Mia's grandfather's cloths on my fingertips, the cries of merchants and customers bargaining in the souk in my ears, the folds of the dresses worn by the Arab women who protected her taking shape here at the kitchen table of the bungalow where Horace and Aida sleep soundly down the hall, resting their tired limbs, their weary hearts, their blemished wrists.

Relations
10/23/2010 7:18 PM

From: mia hakim
To: Ivan Pyefinch

Dear Ivan,
   I had a message from my niece, who is someone I only met once when she was a young girl and now she's a grandmother... She found me again through Facebook and wants to know about her mother, my sister, and I don't know what to say except she looks so much like her. Céline died young, from some kind of cancer, not the same one that killed our mother, but it doesn't matter in the end. Okay... thank you for the new translation. I like it. You must have written it at your cottage. I guess I will see you in two weeks, if you still want me to visit?

The revelations and intimacies in our emails have been one-sided, and even then, filtered through the prism of her film. The idea of her plunging into the morass of my family at the height of Horace's obsessions about the war and Bob, and his crazy flag—what was I thinking? I don't sense Mia is the type to censor herself, even if she agrees to be briefed. Yet I also don't want to deprive myself.

   Of course I want you to come, I write back. Of course I do.

   Each morning without an overnight email from Paris my heart descends a few notches. I want to know how she thinks it will all work out with Karim. Without her translation to distract me, I have no excuse to avoid my paid work—updating the fire safety page for the City of Gatineau website. It makes me wonder if I should buy a rope ladder to hang over the edge of my balcony on the fifth floor. Would I have enough rungs to reach the ground? Would my weight on the ladder keep the hooks around the railings in place or would my swaying body dislodge them? I remember buying Horace a fire extinguisher for Christmas one year. I have a photo of him with it, smiling. The entire cottage is made of wood, even the cedar shake siding was put up in the days before it was fire-retardant. I had thought, for once, he would appreciate this gift. Yet like cards they receive, open, and then return to their envelopes, he pulled it out of the carton, examined it, and then put it back in its box. It is somewhere in the blue garage, its pressure long since dissipated. Maybe, convinced of his miraculous life with Angel Bob on his shoulder, he felt it was unnecessary.

~◉ 23 ◉~

HORACE calls with an update.

"I got another letter from the *Reader's Digest*," he says. "This one has a special promotion for music. Nice music, like the kind we listened to. I thought why the hell not? Live a little. Oh, they installed that box for your computer. It's flashing a lot of lights."

"We can go through it all tonight."

"There's a deadline on this, and I've got to stay in the running."

"I don't think there's a deadline on buying the music."

"It all goes in the same envelope. That's why it's special. I need to do it today. The post office will be closed tomorrow for the parade. I picked up my holster for the flag from the head guy at the Armouries. I'll wear it around my waist, and it'll take the weight of the thing. Everything's coming together. I want to put the flag stand in place before they block off the roads. I'll need your help. That thing is damned heavy."

I wonder if this guy knows the scale of Horace's plan, or

if there's another head guy in charge of the entire parade who's been consulted. They're calling for snow flurries, which will blend nicely with the white paint on the box but possibly do injury to the photocopied page of Horace and Bob secured on the front by Scotch tape.

"I've got a new project. A display of all the planes I flew. I cut them out of that magazine you got me. I'll put it right at the entrance in the hall. Opposite the mirror so you can see it every which way."

Horace chuckles at the thought.

"When are you coming with your friend?"

"It'll just be me."

"She'll miss a hell of a parade."

MIA has been back in Canada for a week, and we've barely written. I was expecting a Skype so we could meet face-to-face virtually. But she wanted to experience me, Horace, and Aida without too much advance research. Now she is stuck in Montreal, unable to arrive this afternoon as planned. She wants me to pick her up at the train station in Brockville tomorrow morning instead. The two of us arriving this evening in Riverton would have been bad enough, but showing up on the day of the parade is not possible. She must know that, which means she has changed her mind, and this must be her way to save face. I told her I won't have time tomorrow. We can meet in Ottawa later in the week. Don't worry about it. They were statements, not questions, but her lack of acknowledgement still left me hanging. I'm disappointed because I can't manage Horace, the flag box, and Aida by myself. I will need to leave her at home during the parade. It will be one less stress for me, except it doesn't feel right.

HORACE has backed the Roadmaster into his driveway so we can pack up the flag stand tomorrow morning without a hernia. With the double-car garage door left wide open and the lights on, I see the flag stand next to the oil drum. He must have heard the forecast because the box is wrapped in a green garbage bag. The tailgate is open, too, with the interior lights shining on the flag in the back of the car. I pull down the garage door and the tailgate, and I am suddenly in darkness.

They're dozing in front of the television and don't hear me come in. Even if they kept the door locked, I would worry about ingratiating salesmen smooth-talking their way inside. He has already bought an air purifier for several thousand dollars that he doesn't know how to work, and I extricated him from a contract for a new gas supplier. The air force flag in the garden sends a message to all and sundry: war veteran lives here! Easy pickings! Once they catch sight of the aircraft display he's planning for the wall in the foyer, he'll be signing up for an alarm system he won't remember to use.

When I came to help out for Halloween, I politely suggested Horace might want to take down the flag for the night. Kids being kids. Out of the question. It was part of his costume. Horace dressed up in his air force uniform complete with his pilot's cap. Rather than affect surprise or interest in the goblins, superheroes, and princesses, he asked them to guess what he was.

Horace's uniform is lovingly draped on a kitchen chair along with a dress shirt and tie. The medals sparkle from the overhead light. His good shoes and socks are within easy reach. On the table, in the egg cup, Aida's evening pills.

I wake him gently.

"You? Here?" he says.

"It's getting late, and you've got a big day tomorrow."

Something Aida might have said to me once, although it may just be a memory from a television show.

"Come on, Aida," he says. "To bed."

"I wasn't sleeping!"

But she has a twinkle in her voice. She puts down her box of clippings, tells me my cheeks are rosy from the cold, and obediently takes the pills with water before padding down the hall after Horace. I go round turning off all the lights, including one downstairs. Unlike in my childhood home, this basement will stay unfinished. It is an expansive space, but the concrete floor is mostly covered with odds and ends. In one corner, near a craft station with more unfinished decoupage projects, two twin beds sit on a round braided carpet that I remember from the 1970s. Horace has turned the area into a second office because his desk under the stairs is covered. On one bed, he's laid three open binders side by side. On the other lie stacks of paper and a three-hole punch—an ongoing project to get his investments in order. I had been planning to put Mia down here. Is it something in the musty atmosphere of this house that clouds the brain?

In the spare room opposite Horace and Aida, I unpack my bag, looking madly for the Blackberry charger. I can see it now clearly plugged into the wall of my condo. Tomorrow morning will be all Horace with no time to find an open store. Riverton takes its Remembrance Day seriously.

I lie awake, listening for sounds of breathing through two doors. My last thought before falling asleep: despite everything, I wish Mia were here.

—◦◎ 24 ◎◦—

HORACE BANGS on my door at seven-thirty, and for a few seconds I am thirteen years old again, getting awakened for an early Saturday morning hockey game. Other fathers made their sons walk to the arena in the dark, duffle bags lashed onto hockey sticks and slung over shoulders. I wanted to be a hobo like my teammates, but couldn't figure out how to do it.

"Look before you pass," Horace would shout, the only parent in the stands at six-fifteen. I wanted to prove him wrong so I continued to throw the puck out blindly from the corner, and then huff in frustration that no one was waiting in the slot.

In later years, he climbed inside the goal judge cage with his Super 8 camera, perching in mid-air to capture any goals I might score. Sitting on the bench, I looked the other way, relieved my glasses had fogged up.

"Your dad's a flag," one of my teammates had said, mumbling through his mouth guard.

"A flag?"

"A fag, stupid."

My wrist shot actually lifted off the ice. It squeaked between the goalie's shoulder and the crossbar, forcing overtime in the playoffs. They cheered my heroics, but I was aiming for Horace.

I could never compete with his good skin, his athletic prowess, his overbearing self-confidence. Even in his sixties, he whipped me at tennis in Florida. I ran around the court, trying to return his volleys. He barely broke a sweat.

"Wait for the ball to come closer to the ground," he'd said. He grinned at my frustration at this late advice. He was like the carny who once gave me tips on shooting ducks after I had spent my shells.

Horace liked reducing any movement to its bare essentials, while basking in the glow of an appreciative and preferably female audience. He befriended a widow outside their retirement park who couldn't handle all her windfall grapefruit. Horace gallantly offered to help, sweeping up the best ones like errant tennis balls. I held the bag.

It wasn't just the picking. He had better ways to eat the grapefruit as well.

"What I do is peel them, mix them all up, and put them right in the fridge," he remarked. "You get it all done ahead of time, so then you just reach in, and it's there when you want it."

Sure enough, the next morning, I opened the refrigerator and the mush was there, just like he said. It was like wanting corn-on-the-cob only to find it's been creamed, but his face was so full of pride that I could only grin at his clever invention.

HORACE never buys grapefruit in Canada until prices drop in January so I content myself with a glass of orange juice. The frozen kind, like everything else here except breakfast food and his beloved carrot muffins. He hasn't taken time to stir it up properly so it's lumpy. What pours out in my glass is too thin, but I drink it uncomplaining. There are children starving in China. He's so anxious to get downtown that he's not even using his favourite bowl and spoon for his cereal. Normally he washes them by hand so they're not lost in the dishwasher for days on end. With all his last-minute preparations for the parade, they must be sitting dirty in the sink.

His uniform, draped over the back of the chair, seems so at home I want to put out another place setting. I know him enough not to attempt small talk. Taking of cereal is a sacred ritual not to be interrupted. Combine that with the anticipation of the parade and any unneeded words from me will not go over well. If he had cooked eggs, I'd be walking on the shells.

With a mouth full of Corn Flakes, Horace calls to Aida, who is sitting with a mug of tea in the sunroom that opens from the kitchen.

"Don't forget the waist," he says.

"Right."

She gets up, moving toward the kitchen, and then points to the chair.

"Horace has his uniform out, did you see?"

"It's the big parade today," I tell her. "We're going downtown with his flag, and then coming back so he can change."

"That will be nice."

"The waist, Aida!"

Why has he left this to the last minute? He's probably been on Aida to let out the waist since Halloween. No matter how much he sucked it up, he couldn't manage the last button.

Aida walks to the sink and pulls out the garbage from behind the cupboard door. Waste. Horace doesn't notice or else misses the homonym.

"You could leave the last button undone," I tell him.

"Hurry up with your food. It's after eight. I'll open the car."

He jumps from the table nearly knocking Aida onto the floor with the garbage.

"It's not even half full. What's your rush? Don't forget my pants."

He takes the bag with him to the foyer, leaves it on the floor while he puts on his shoes and fall jacket, and then heads out the front door without it.

"Horace wants you to let out his pants. Do you have

needle and thread?"

"In the drawer underneath the knives and forks," she says.

Remarkably, despite all odds, they're exactly where she says they are. There's no time to cajole her into eating breakfast and taking her pills. The best I can do is guide her back to the wicker chair, leave the pants and sewing tools in her lap, and hope for the best.

Horace has got the tailgate and garage door open. Together we heave that box of bricks into the back of the Roadmaster, and set off. At this hour, Highway 2 is clear of traffic, and we drive right up to the Cenotaph. We're so early that no one's around to stop us, but there are no mic stands or speakers either. Horace walks straight up to the spot just in front of the statue. Like pirates with ill-gotten booty, we haul our box of treasure, still in its garbage bag, to its anointed place. All we're missing are the pickaxes to break through the cement to dig our hole.

"You're sure you want to leave it here?" I ask him. "Once they get set up, it might be in the way."

"They can move around it."

"You cleared all this with the head guy, right?"

"Don't bug me."

No sense arguing with him. The flurries are getting wetter so there's no sense removing the bag either. In the rear-view mirror, I can see this green monstrosity in the hallowed space of the Cenotaph. When the set-up crew arrives, will they call for the police dogs? They might try to move it, sense its immense weight, and give up. Or they might wait for the head guy in case it has some symbolic importance that escapes them.

It's close to nine by the time we're back home.

"I hope to hell Aida has those pants fixed."

"If she hasn't, it won't kill you not to do up the button."

"Don't tell me what to do."

I watch him stride purposefully into the sunroom where he is sure to find the pants sitting on Aida's lap covered in scraps of butterflies and birds.

"Who the hell are you?" Horace says.

It's Mia. She puts down her tea and stands up. Is it out of courtesy or fear? Fear, because her hand is shaking. Maybe she wants to keep Horace from towering over her. From the photos on the web I thought Mia was taller, but she looks about five foot four—a good foot shorter than Horace, even if his spine is curving forward. Everything else is how I pictured except she's so much more intense in person—the wild frizzy hair and dangling earrings, the leopard-skin jacket and a scarf, eyeliner and dark lipstick, a whiff of perfume. It's no wonder she worries about going back to Tunisia, especially if her fear is so transparent.

I make quick introductions, suggesting Mia has come all the way from Paris to be here on Remembrance Day.

"Paris!"

"Did you let out my pants?"

"Oh those pants! It won't take me a minute."

"I'll give you two minutes."

"Excuse me, Horace," Mia says. "It's not a hard job, taking out the seam, but it will take at least fifteen minutes."

"What's she saying?"

"She says it will take longer than you've got. You'll just have to leave the button undone."

Mia picks up the pants, and hands them to Horace.

"Put on your pants," she says. "I'll help you make them fit."

"What?"

"Mia will help you. Just get your pants on."

Mia is speaking louder, but her accent continues to throw Horace. Not only am I her translator, I've become an interpreter as well.

As Mia looks on in alarm, Horace starts pulling off his everyday trousers in the middle of the sunroom. She walks over and kisses me on either cheek.

"You got my message?" she asks.

"No, my phone is dead. How did you find us?"

"You are the only Pyefinch in this town."

"Where are my socks?"

"I'll help you find them, dear."

"Never mind. They're in my shoes."

"I can't believe you're here," I tell her. "You have no idea what you're getting into."

"I have an idea. It's very special here. Your mother is adorable."

"If you could stay with her while I take Horace downtown."

"You see," he says. "I can't get the last button."

"You help him with his shirt and tie and I will help your mother get dressed," Mia says. "Then I will fix the pants."

Ten minutes later Mia emerges with a leather belt.

"The pants are too tight. The last thing I need is a belt."

Without a word, Mia threads the belt through the hoops and clamps it shut over the offending button.

"*Voilà!*"

"You can't see the button!" Horace says. "*Merci beaucoup.*"

"*Vous parlez français ! Quand même!*"

"He knows a few swear words, too," I say.

Mia disappears again to finish helping Aida, and I sit Horace down in a kitchen chair to put on his shoes and socks. His declining flexibility combined with the stiff wool pants make it hard for him to bend over. Afterwards, I help him on with his air force jacket and the holster. He walks up and down the hall a few times pretending he's got the flag.

"How are we doing for time?" he asks.

"We have about ten minutes."

"Then I'll sit down."

Whenever fatigue trumps anxiety for Horace I start to worry. He sits on the sofa, slouching until his neck is supported by a pillow, and closes his eyes. I fix Aida some cereal and get her pills, while Mia whispers:

"Her hair is really dirty."

"There's a hat in the hall closet on the top shelf."

"Do I have time for her makeup?"

"I don't know where she keeps it."

"I have mine."

Her hand is still shaking.

"It's okay," I tell her. "You can relax. They don't bite."

"I'm not afraid. I'm cold."

Horace is still dozing so I hold up my hand to indicate five minutes. Mia gives me a high five against my open palm. She uses the hand that's not cold.

"This war thing, this flag, is everything I hate, but I will lie for you."

It takes longer to get out the door than I anticipate, and then to get Horace's body to bend onto the passenger seat beside me. Mia and Aida sit behind us, separated by the long part of the flagpole that extends to the dashboard through the centre of the car.

I tear down Highway 2 to make up for lost time. Both Horace and Mia doze, lulled to sleep by the motion of the Roadmaster. With the stylish winter hat I bought for her last Christmas, the lipstick, and a dash of colour on her cheeks, Aida looks ready for a parade.

They're setting up pylons to block the road when we

approach City Hall. Horace and Mia wake as the car slows down and then stops.

"Oh no," Horace says. "We're too late to get through."

The anguish in his voice breaks my heart, as if I'm the father of a young boy who has lost his innocence too soon.

A youngish policeman is motioning for me to turn around. Before I can get the window down, Mia is out of the car, flashing a smile, pointing to Horace and the flag in the back, and making little pleading gestures. The cop has no chance against this attack of charm. He walks round to Horace's side, and helps him out of the car. I pull out the pole, assemble the flag, and help him get it in the holster.

"It's a hell of a weight all the same," he says.

"You going to be all right with that, sir?" the cop says.

His spirits revived, Horace salutes him with his free hand. He walks carefully to the steps of City Hall where other veterans are waiting for the order to get into formation. A few are wearing gabardine coats and gloves for warmth, but most, like Horace, are toughing it out in their winter uniforms and bare hands.

Well-wishers are already taking spots on the sidewalk along Main Street. I point Mia toward the Cenotaph at the end of the parade route, and encourage them to get as close as possible to see Horace plant his flag.

By the time I park the car and get to the Cenotaph, it's almost ten-fifteen. The flurries have stopped and the sun has come out, which is miraculous. But the flag stand has been moved behind the Cenotaph in front of the provincial flags to make way for the podium and sound equipment. Technicians are testing the microphone levels, while a couple of veterans are huddled in discussion with a clergyman. I'm not sure whether one of them is the head guy, but clearly, this is not going according to Horace's plan. I should have pushed him harder for what he was told, or checked myself. Now I need to make the best of this mess, and I'm divided between embarrassment that I'll be the one, literally, holding the bag, and my rage that I agreed to come at all.

It's easier to rip the bag open than try to lift an edge of the box on my own and wriggle it out of the bag. Fortunately for Horace, the photocopied picture of him and Bob is on the panel of the box facing outward, toward the crowd. If this had been done by a nine-year-old girl, it might be touching or cute. Instead, it's pathetic, and my anger toward Horace starts getting redirected toward my role in letting this show go on.

"This belongs to you?"

It's one of the veterans from the other side of the Cenotaph.

"Not really. It belongs to my father. I'm just helping out."

I give him my best winning grin, but it's met with a scowl and a shaking hand that points to the other flags behind me. He's probably cold and angry.

"I told him he can't plant his damned flag up here."

"So why did you put this here with the other flags?"

"Because it was too damned heavy to move anywhere else. There's a protocol. No flag can be higher than the provincial flags. You need to move it across the street."

He sees my eyes drop to his hand. He's no longer pointing, but it still shakes.

"I'm not afraid. I'm just cold. But you're afraid of your father. I can tell."

I want to break protocol again, put this man in his place. Except I wonder if the shaking isn't an illness of some kind, which may be colouring his response. Then again Mia was shaking from the cold right in our house. I don't lash out because this guy is right: I am afraid of Horace. Not to disobey him so much but rather to disappoint him.

"It's too heavy for me to move by myself."

"Then leave the damned thing. He can plant his flag after the ceremony. Not before. After all the wreaths are laid."

"I'm sure that will be fine."

"I don't care if it's fine."

He shakes a little as he walks now, and I feel bad I've aggravated him. In any case, it makes sense for Horace to wait until after the service. I only worry the flag may get heavy to hold. It's not the weight so much, it's how long he has to carry it.

Both sides of the sidewalk have filled up fast, and I scan the crowd for Mia and Aida. They're standing in front of the photocopy shop. The manager of the store, true to his promise, is out there as well, which makes me think all is unfolding as it should, even if I can't see the whole picture. It's not the best spot for them because while they are facing the Cenotaph, they'll be staring at Horace's back for the entire service. I decide to stay on this side of the street so I can keep an eye on Horace. I squeeze into the line behind the rows of chairs set out for veterans in wheelchairs and walkers, or those simply too weak to march.

The band is starting to play and the men are falling in line. I can see Horace's flag towering above all the heads. As they march, the crowd cheers and waves tiny Canadian flags. Horace's face is steely, determined. He won't fail Bob.

The troupe makes it down King Street to the Cenotaph without mishap. Horace is toward the back but towers over everyone with his flag. The scowly veteran gives a short speech and the clergyman follows with a sermon. Up the hill, at eleven o'clock, the town clock marks out the time. No flypast or twenty-one gun salute, only a moment of silence. The wreath laying takes forever with every business, civic club, and school determined to honour dead veterans by making the remaining live ones stand interminably in the cold. At least it's not snowing.

When the formation finally breaks up around eleven-twenty, Horace moves deliberately toward the Cenotaph. If anything, he seems renewed rather than drained by the experience. His step seems more assured than usual, although I'm waiting for the other shoe to drop once he sees the box has been moved behind the monument. With the crew moving in swiftly to take down the equipment, veterans greeting their families and saying goodbye to friends, and children swarming to see the wreaths close-up, Horace has plenty of potential obstacles. I'm standing in the square next to the flag stand to help him get his bearings. He sees me and smiles proudly. A few more steps and he'll make it. He doesn't seem put off that the box is at the back. Mia and Aida arrive in time to see him lift the flagpole from the holster. Slowly, with great deliberation, he slides the pole into the hollow pipe. He takes a few steps back and salutes. Some children come up to him and ask for photos with him and the flag. Afterwards, I seat him down in one of the vacated chairs so he can rest while I fetch the car.

"*Magnifique!*"

Mia kisses him on either cheek and Horace positively glows. Local businesses are offering free coffee and tea to veterans in uniform, but this show of gratitude doesn't move Horace. The parade was it.

Once home, his uniform hung up for another year, he slouches down on the couch to doze, while Mia and I have a chance to greet each other properly for the first time. It feels superfluous. It seems the most natural thing in the world that she should be poking her head into the refrigerator and cupboards in search of food. She must feel more comfortable because she's stopped shaking.

"There is nothing fresh, except these muffins and some cheese," she says.

"Soup and crackers would be fine."

"*La grande cuisine.*"

I'm not sure if she's making fun of them, me, or the situation.

"We'll head back to Ottawa after lunch. You must be tired, too. Leaving so early from Montreal."

Mia looks concerned, asks if they will be all right on their own. It's a question I ask myself constantly. For her I present a veneer of confidence in their ability to cope. It works because she immediately shifts into talking about her meeting tomorrow, and her planned research trip to Tunisia in a few weeks.

Horace wakes up and lets everyone know with a huge yawn. He stumbles a little getting to the table, his legs still weak from the morning march. Aida happily joins us at the table, attracted by the presence of Mia.

"Ahellofamorning"

His words blur together, as if he's leaving a rushed message on a pay phone to avoid the long-distance charge.

--◦◉) 25 ◉◦--

I BRING HORACE to the hospital, thinking it may only be a mini-stroke, like the one he had in Florida. The doctors will give him the once over, slap him on the back for the scare he gave everyone, and send us on our way. He'll plant his flag in the garden and stand arm-in-arm while Mia and I head off to Ottawa in our rental. Maybe he'll give a salute.

But Horace is not coming home tonight. They send him in an ambulance to the Kingston General, an hour away, where they have stroke specialists. I drive back to the house to let Mia know I'm going to follow the ambulance.

"I'm sorry about this," I tell her. "You don't need to stay."

But it's a lie and Mia knows it. If she had not shown up unexpectedly, what would I have done? Bring Aida with me to Kingston, I guess.

"We will be fine, just us girls."

I hand Mia the keys to the Roadmaster in case she has an emergency with Aida. She shakes her head.

"I don't know how to drive."

So many things I don't know about Mia. For Aida, it all makes sense—how she opened the front door to a strange woman who got her dressed, made her up, accompanied her to the parade, fixed her lunch, and will keep her company this evening. Of course her mind hasn't retained anything of what's happened today. It's enough there is someone here, warm and affectionate, who is kind to her.

KAREN and I took Horace and Aida out for dinner in Kingston for their fiftieth wedding anniversary. I had chosen the restaurant, in part, for the pianist who played easy listening classics. I primed him to play a few old-time favourites to stir up Horace's feelings. Except Horace said they made him think of Bob. Aida didn't react, so used to her secondary role. Karen sat stone-faced until the two of us drove home to Ottawa later that evening. She couldn't sit still, turning every few moments in the dark to launch another tirade against Horace. She suggested his projected feelings maybe went further than he realized, and that Bob was the true love of his life. I didn't defend Horace or side with Karen. It felt like a useless debate, and my refusal to take a position only enraged her more. Choose your battles was never Karen's rallying cry. She could fight on several fronts at once, giving equal credence to perceived slights and real grievances. She interpreted my silence as tacit acceptance of Horace's boorish behaviour. More than that, it opened previously sealed wounds about my own slip-ups toward her for which I thought the statute of limitations had long expired. It wasn't long after that she took up with P'tit-Luc. It's stupid, I know, but I trace the demise of my marriage to that evening in Kingston. Ever since then, I've disliked the place.

I have a cousin who is a nurse at the Kingston General—a niece of Aida's—whom I haven't seen in years. I can't remember her married name and don't think I would recognize her. These are the moments I regret the frayed bonds with Aida's family, the unspoken reasons for distance with her remaining brother and sister and any other sibling I may not have heard about. My cousin may have left this hospital years ago. I tend to think of people with whom I've lost contact as living outside of time. They do not move or change jobs so when I chance upon their last known whereabouts they will be exactly as I left them. Maybe that therapist was right about my relationship with cupboard doors. I really do think I can come back later to close them.

A nurse who is not my cousin tells me that Horace has had a bona fide stroke. He may be here a while. I poke my nose behind the curtain to find Horace sitting up in the bed. His eyes are open, but he's not able to get any words out—for the first time in his life.

"They're going to keep you overnight," I tell him.

He nods, which I take as a good sign.

"You know you're in Kingston? They have specialists here."

I can't bring myself to use the "s" word.

"We'll make sure you get your money's worth."

He grins, a little lopsided maybe, but he clearly understands.

"I'm heading home, but I'll be back tomorrow with Aida."

He squeezes my hand, and I kiss him quickly before any tears from me short-circuit the wires in his chest. As I turn for a last wave, he gives me a salute. Another good sign except it reminds me how he helped lift the flag box into the car after the parade. I couldn't have found someone else to help me?

IT'S about six o'clock and already dark by the time I pull into the driveway of the bungalow. Mia has flipped on the outside light, and the lights of the living room are also lit, which never happens. It feels both foreign and familiar. I think of evenings as a five-year-old kneeling backward on the pink couch in our Ottawa home, my eyes peeled for a sign of Horace walking up the hill after work and expecting dinner on the table.

The rock garden is in shadow, and seems vacant without the flag in place. I will leave it in the back of the Roadmaster until Horace is ready to come home.

Mia hears the door and rushes up to me in the foyer.

"Your mother is upset. She keeps asking about your father. I can't say anything to make her feel better."

"I'll talk to her."

"It was fine for a long time then she got jealous."

Mia adds a laugh, but her voice catches all the same. I don't ask what was said. I kiss her on each cheek, in the French way, and she draws me in for a hug. Her fingers dig slightly into my back and then let go. So much has happened today and it's not over yet. We still have to work out sleeping arrangements.

Aida looks up from her chair with the cuttings and smiles.

"Horace is off somewhere," she says.

As Mia passes behind me into the kitchen, Aida waves me in closer so she can whisper in my ear.

"There's a girl here."

"That's Mia. She's making us some dinner."

"Oh is that it?"

Her hushed conspiratorial voice gives way to a laugh that releases her tension. I join Mia in the kitchen where she is going through cupboards. I didn't have time to buy fresh food.

"You want to eat now? It's not even six-thirty," Mia says. "And there's nothing in the fridge but these horrible boxes."

"Welcome to Riverton."

I instruct Mia in the art of fine dining at the Pyefinch home after she can't squeeze three boxes of Stouffer's meatloaf into the microwave.

"What is that on your wrist?" she asks.

"The image of a silver dollar."

I hold it up so she can see the two figures in the canoe.

"You wanted a tattoo on your wrist?" she says. "Your father talks non-stop about the war. Don't you know anything about history?"

"It was my declaration of independence from Horace."

"How's that working out for you?"

After less than a day in Riverton, Mia has the cadence of a native speaker and the timing of a stand-up comic.

As she reaches to shut the cupboard door, her silver bracelets ride up her right arm and I catch a glimpse of her own history on her wrist.

AIDA picks at her food, conscious again of Horace's absence. I tell her he had an accident, and they're keeping him overnight in the hospital, but everything will be fine. "We'll see him first thing tomorrow."

"We can't go now?"

"He's tired out, and visiting hours are over."

I repeat this message a few times over the evening in between bad television shows, and more cutting out of flowers and butterflies. At eight o'clock, Mia's phone rings and she disappears into the kitchen for a few minutes. I don't hear a conversation and I wonder if she's whispering to Karim about how she's landed in this crazy family.

At bedtime, despite my teasing and cajoling, Aida is refusing her bedtime pill. Mia pours a glass of Perrier, retrieves her purse, and sits down beside her on the sofa.

"Aida, can I show you something? Look at the picture on this little box."

"A butterfly! How beautiful! What is it?"

"I keep my pills in here. See? I have to take one now before bed. Oh, look! You have a pill to take, too. It's so boring. Maybe we can do it together! Except I need to take mine with fizzy water."

Mia puts the pill in Aida's palm and clinks her glass, which makes Aida laugh. She swallows her pill without further protest, as if it's the most natural thing in the world.

Close to eleven, with Aida settled in bed, I sit with Mia in the living room on the furniture that had been in storage for twenty years. She sits in a white wing-backed chair, and I sit on the same couch from my childhood where I used to wait for my father to come home. Both of them are so well used that the stuffing has all but disappeared.

I tell her everything the doctors said, which is not much, and which I already wrote her about. Her leg is shaking again.

"I can stay with your mother for a few weeks, until I go to Tunisia."

"You don't need to do that."

"I want to. Unless you don't want me to."

"No, of course not. It would be a great help."

We fall silent. Too many unknowns to fathom. Too much intimacy thrust on us too quickly. She looks over at me.

"Can I sit beside you?"

Without waiting for an answer, which would have been Yes, Mia sidles up next to me. Her perfume, while not strong, quickly starts giving me a headache. Or perhaps it's just the tension of the day catching up. But still I become fixated on the scent, as if it's the most important consideration in where we sleep tonight. It keeps me from falling completely into a fantasy of pressing my body against hers in bed. Even so, the idea of Mia's softness and curves is pushing away the memory of Karen's leanness. Having only ever been with Karen, her taut body had become my default ideal. I had never been attracted to what they used to call full-figured women. But I am drawn to Mia, her wild clothes, her exotic scent, her carefully constructed dishevelled look. Even her skin, with its darker hue, is different. Beyond all this, she has a good heart.

Karim will help her research the film. Through this intimate process of re-discovery, she will also reconcile with him. What they started in Montreal years ago will resume in new form. If she doesn't convince him to come back to Canada, she will return to Tunisia. I see it so clearly, and how what happens in this bungalow could change everything. I can't see how she could make the film without him. I can only hope that Karim blows his chance after she no longer needs him, but I don't want to be the instrument of his undoing.

Mia and I sit in silence, our arms and shoulders touching. The sensation relaxes me, but sets her arm shaking again.

"We should go to bed," she says.

"You can have the guest room. I'll sleep out here."

"On this? It's so hard."

"There are beds in the basement, too."

"I do not sleep in basements."

I hold back a laugh at her seriousness. She gets up, arms folded in schoolmarm fashion. Maybe to hide her trembling.

"The bed in the bedroom is big enough for two people, but you do what you want."

She gets up, shakes my hand in faux seriousness.

"*Bonne nuit, Monsieur.*"

I WAKE around four in the morning seated on the couch from where I've apparently been sleeping. My neck aches from the weight of my bowed head and my eyes blink from the blazing lights of the living room. No trace of Mia's scent remains.

She has left the light on in the bathroom, for me or for her. I don't see a sign of life from the crack under her door so I return to the couch, not bothering to undress or get blankets. It's warm enough without. If Horace only knew the furnace has been blazing all night.

At breakfast, Mia is distant at first, bustling around the kitchen, unaware that Aida won't eat anything until at least nine-thirty. Yet, once again, Mia succeeds. Not only does Aida eat her cereal, but she also takes her morning pills on time. The butterfly box once again does the trick. Except this time Mia takes four or five pills. I want to know why, but it seems indiscreet to ask.

In what I take as her natural disposition to not hold a grudge, Mia teases me about my wrinkled shirt. Unlike her, I didn't bring a suitcase full of clothes. Today she is wearing black leggings, a blouse, and a frilly skirt topped with a yellow scarf—a combination that fills Aida with admiration. Together they disappear into Aida's room to come up with an outfit suitable for visiting Horace in the hospital.

En route, we're quiet in the car until Mia's phone rings at eleven. I realize the sound is not an incoming call but rather an alarm. She opens her butterfly box, and takes her pills with fizzy water. Then she falls asleep again, lulled by the motion.

We discover Horace has been transferred to the stroke unit on the seventh floor where he is dozing in a semi-private room. The other bed is empty, which is both reassuring and foreboding. Mia takes Aida for tea while I search out a nurse for an update.

The stroke was mild, she says. It's affected his ability to process information and communicate. It's too soon to say if it will affect his balance or judgment. What he needs most right now is rest. We should keep our visit short and ask Yes or No questions.

Mia hangs back while I bring Aida into the room to see Horace. He is pleased to see her, but quickly gets aggravated by her smothering kisses. I play language cop, answering her repetitive "How are you?" questions, and interpreting the missing or misplaced words coming out of Horace's mouth. Five minutes of this is all I judge Horace can stand so I announce he has to rest.

It's Friday, which means I should stick around for an update on Horace before the regular staff head home for the weekend. This will mean constantly distracting Aida, which will be exhausting. I could bring Mia and Aida back to Riverton and return to the hospital. Or I could bring them as far as the cottage where they could spend the afternoon with Margaret, which would save me an hour of travel time. There is also the question of the rental car, which is due back in Ottawa at five o'clock. Maybe I could return it in Brockville and pay a penalty. I could take over the Roadmaster until Horace comes home. My name is still on the insurance. Far from overwhelming me, these logistical questions fix my attention on the Yes or No. How I will manage continued visits here with Aida, how the two of them will cope on their own if Horace is disabled, how Mia's presence simplifies and complicates matters—these questions are more likely to overtax my brain if I think about them too much.

After lunch in the cafeteria and another short visit with Horace, a nurse reassures me about the weekend staff. She is Black, the only person of colour on the floor. Despite the kindness that radiates from her face, I wonder how Horace will react. Will he ask where she's from?

"We'll take good care of your father, don't worry. How is your mother coping?"

"She has Alzheimer's so she doesn't really understand."

"So he was the primary caregiver?"

Her head turns ever so slightly and she changes the weight of her feet. Her voice, too, has a different tone. Less assured.

"I'll make note of that," she says. "It will be a few days before the team assesses him. Not before Monday."

This news washes out her previous assurances about weekend care.

"But how do you think he's doing?"

"I've seen worse. Already his language is coming back. It's hard to say about everything else."

"You mean how he walks, his balance?"

"A stroke can affect everything. Moods, judgment. Everything."

"Like his ability to drive, that sort of thing?"

She takes two steps back to get a good look at me, as if she can't believe what she heard.

"He won't be driving any time soon. This is hard for a lot of seniors, especially men. If you think that's going to be a problem, we need to tell the doctor. He'll write to the ministry. Is your father attached to his car?"

26

I CHECK THE OIL of the Roadster before breakfast, anxious about the stress of daily travel to Kingston. In my head I'm singing the old song about the grandfather clock on the shelf that strikes one last time when the old man dies. Maybe as long as I can keep this car ticking, its owner will stay alive too.

Every morning we visit Horace, eat lunch in the cafeteria, and visit him again. I confer with whatever member of the rehab team I can find for updates, which are better each day. In mid-afternoon we drive home, and Mia prepares a snack. She has adjusted to the six o'clock dinner hour in Riverton but otherwise expands our horizons with Middle-Eastern dishes like cous-cous and tajine. Aida helps prepare the meals, which occupies her time more meaningfully and stimulates her mind. By the time the food is served, she has forgotten the menu but enjoys everything all the same. In the evening, I watch bad TV with Aida, while Mia writes to Karim to finalize her trip. At night, Mia sleeps with Aida, giving me the second bedroom. I could almost get used to the routine.

Now that we're spending so much time together, I notice Mia takes her pills in the morning and at bedtime like Aida. But her phone alarm also rings with reminders to take them at eleven, two, five, and eight. She carries food and a drink in her purse at all times. Sometimes she shakes, sometimes not. Aida's regimen seems manageable in comparison.

The oil seems fine, although there's no telling what else could suddenly go wrong. In a half hour, our first caregiver will arrive. I want to see how Aida will cope in our absence so when the doorbell rings Mia slips into the spare room and I head down to the basement.

Aida lets in the caregiver, but they walk by the stairwell too quickly for me to see her face. From her voice I can tell she's young, maybe in her twenties. Her voice is whiny and insistent, irritated in less than ten minutes at Aida's repetitions and lack of interest in breakfast. Then all is quiet. I creep up the stairs to find Aida in her wicker chair cutting out butterflies, and the caregiver—who looks like she's skipping eleventh grade—texting on her iPhone from the chair opposite. She jumps when she sees me standing there. Then she smiles, hoping that will smooth things over.

"I think you might as well go now," I tell her.

"I tried giving her some breakfast. She said she wasn't hungry."

"Did you read my note?"

She blushes, looks around for it, and shrugs helplessly.

"It's on the kitchen table," I tell her. "How long have you been doing this?"

"I'm really sorry, sir. Really I am. I really need this job. Please give me another chance."

"What's happening?"

It's Mia, coming up from behind me now, and making me jump.

"He wants to fire me. I said I was sorry. They didn't tell me there was a note."

"What did she do?" Mia asks.

"Nothing," I say. "That's the point."

"I was going to try again. She didn't want to eat. You are so unfair."

"I'm never very hungry first thing in the morning," Aida says.

"You see? Please don't tell my boss. Can we just say I was here for the full hour?"

When I don't respond, she fights back tears, grabs her bag at the foot of the wicker chair, and brushes by us. I watch her jam her feet into running shoes in two swift motions, grab her jacket, and leave. She doesn't slam the door. I wish she had. It would make me feel less crappy.

"You're not really going to report her?" Mia asks.

"I don't know. She was texting."

"So get someone else, but don't make it harder for her. You don't know her story."

Mia's voice has an edge I haven't heard before.

"So when are we going?" she asks.

"After lunch. Meals on Wheels is coming in an hour."

"So we'll only see your father once today."

"I don't know."

"Can we at least go to your cottage today?"

"If the sun is out."

"Ivan is something, isn't he?" Mia says to Aida. "He never says Yes or No."

Aida laughs, and I take advantage of her good humour to give her the morning pills.

MIA is working on her laptop in the dining room when the doorbell rings at noon. I playfully, but firmly, pull her up from the chair and escort her to the stairs. She stops at the top, an edge of fear in her voice.

"You go down. You don't need me to watch them. I will stay in the bedroom."

She walks away before I can respond, leaving me to descend on my own. Slowly. I should really get Horace to install a railing before someone breaks their neck.

Aida invites the stranger into the house, leading her to the kitchen with the mysterious package. The Meals on Wheels volunteer turns down the offer of tea, and Aida sees her back to the door. The whole encounter is over within thirty seconds.

I follow Aida when she goes back to her chair in the sunroom, leaving the hot meal covered in foil on the kitchen counter, forgotten.

WE arrive at the hospital just as a nurse is putting Horace to bed after some walking practice. I run after the occupational therapist, a sporty looking blonde who is breezing down the hall with a chart, her ponytail flipping back and forth from the apparent wind. She probably drinks kombucha on her breaks and goes sailing at lunch hour. Mia catches up to us in time to hear that Horace is recovering well. In another week, he will be ready to come home. I should be happy, but my first thought is to wonder where Mia will sleep.

"Your father seems to think he's going to drive himself home," she says. "We've tried to explain, but he's not processing information very well."

"This is normal, no?" Mia says. "Isn't that why he's here?

His trouble is with the brain."

The woman ignores Mia's comment, smiles at me, and pulls herself up even straighter.

"If you think the driving will be a problem, we can ask the doctor to send a letter to the ministry."

"I'll let you know."

Mia grabs my arm on the way back to Horace's room.

"I don't like this woman. She has no heart. You don't want to denounce him to the government."

Again, the edge in Mia's voice. The same one I heard this morning when she asked me not to report the caregiver.

"I don't know what I'll do."

"She had you eating out of her hand. You'll do what she wants."

Mia pushes ahead, arriving back to the room a few steps in front of me. Aida is curled up in bed with Horace, smothering him with kisses and promising to take care of him.

"How are you?" she asks him.

"I just told you."

"We'd better leave Horace to rest now. We'll see him tomorrow. And he'll be coming home soon."

"My God, you are such a control freak," Mia says, hissing the words in my ear and storming off.

Aida gives Horace another kiss, which he shakes off. At the door, Aida waves and Horace calls me back.

"The next time you come, you don't need to bring Aida."

MIA is silent in the back seat all the way to the cottage, a forty-minute drive. I fill up the space with commentary about the St. Lawrence River and the Thousand Islands, as if I'm a guide on one of the boat tours. When we stop at a gas station, Mia buys junk food to help her pills go down.

With the water shut down, we bring Aida to Margaret's house for the bathroom, and she stays for a visit. This is the first time Mia and I have been alone together during the day, and we have only one hour left of sunlight. I'm wishing now I hadn't put the shutters up yet because the cottage looks so forlorn. The main patio is covered in more leaves and small branches nipped off by the squirrels for the acorns. All the lawn furniture has been stored so she brushes off a spot on the edge of the patio, sits down, and stares at the river. Her hand shakes. I stand off to one side, pretending not to notice.

"I'm leaving tomorrow. I need to do some things in Montreal before my flight."

"Okay."

"You don't care if I go."

In my head, I am already struggling to get Aida dressed in the morning and find the right shade of lipstick. Without Mia, I will need to take her with me to the hospital, despite Horace's wishes. Without Mia, there will be no buffer when Horace comes home. But these are side benefits of Mia's presence. The real meaning of her departure is not something I am ready to dwell on.

"Not true."

"*Tu ne veux pas parler en français un peu?*"

We switch to French, and her words become more fluid and mine more deliberate. I don't mind. It's easier to speak of difficult things in French. I don't feel the words in the same way.

"Of course I want you to stay longer," I tell her. "But you've got your own life." What I don't say: we hardly know each other, but I want you to stay.

"You are too wrapped up in your parents," she says, in English.

"They need me."

A leaf falls in her hair, and she shakes it off.

"I hate nature."

"Why did you want to come to the cottage?"

"To see it."

I sit beside her on the patio. Our shoulders brush up against one another. If another leaf falls, it will hit us both at once.

She links her arm around mine, and I think: would it be so wrong to think of myself for once, and not her film in Tunisia or her love for Karim? To kiss her, for instance. She has not been wearing perfume. I'm not sure if she's adapting to life in Riverton or is merely sensitive to the scent-free rules in the hospital. Maybe she's just run out. Yet sitting this close to her for the first time, I realize she has a scent all the same, especially when she speaks, as if her words gain flavour in her mouth before they are released. I sense her arm shaking, and she does as well, and she breaks away.

"Is something wrong?"

"If you want to know something important about me, ask about my films."

We sit on the patio in silence, the cold stones and her flash of anger amplifying our discomfort. I am about to ask about her films when Margaret approaches, arm-in-arm with Aida, and I turn my attention to her.

—◦ 27 ◦—

BY MUTUAL agreement, Mia and I share the spare room. We are under the covers, stripped to underclothes, the bedside lamp on low because Mia is afraid of the dark and I am afraid of the light. Words spill out of us in English and French. We speak of spins from the sky and flights to the sea, of the scent of a hockey arena and a souk at dawn, of wrists marked for life by a needle and a razor blade, of involuntary movement and inertia.

—◉ 28 ◉—

THE MORNING LIGHT of late November is faint through the sheers, yet strong enough to illuminate Mia's naked face turned toward me, her eyes still closed in sleep. Without makeup and with hair falling unchecked over her cheek, Mia seems raw and vulnerable. Without the multiple bracelets on her arm I can see the three lines on her wrist that never quite healed from what she called a folly of youth. Her arms and legs are still. When she wakes, they will be stiff or shaking uncontrollably until she takes medication. She does not name her illness because, she says, that gives it more power. My Sickness, she calls it, and I hear a capital letter. She is still in the honeymoon phase. After ten years it will get worse. Not many people know the truth. She is afraid producers will not give her money to make films. Maybe, I think, Mia will beat the odds like Aida did with her blood condition.

Waking to the aftermath of sex might have been easier than to these emotional intimacies. In a week she will be sleeping with Karim. I like to think it will only be physical, that she doesn't share her deepest self with him. Not that I share much with her about me. It's much easier to speak through the filter of Horace and Aida than to take my own space. With Karen, all our shared history seemed to void the need to talk about our inner worlds. We hid them even from ourselves. Speaking with Mia, I start to recognize my own DNA in stories I had long told as a bemused observer—the echo of Aida's silence and sacrifice in my ellipses, the grandiosity of Horace in my resolve to keep my parents on an even keel. What has come of it, what stays with me this morning, is a sense of exposure. The fear is not so much about what I have said. More about what slipped out without my knowing, and what is expected of me now. I want her to stay. So she can care for Aida or so I can care for her? I wonder if Karim knows about her Sickness.

We will stay close to home today before Mia takes the train to Montreal. Since Horace doesn't want to see Aida at the hospital, it works out better this way. I can't tell them the truth. Either Mia would despise Horace for treating his wife so poorly or she would despise me for snitching on him. I did ask her what's been bothering me about our work together. It seemed premature, the translation. There was no flow to it. And I didn't understand why she even needed it in English. She admitted our exchanges were all about getting her head clear. Sharing her thoughts with someone completely outside of her life experience, and seeing her words in another language, allows her a different perspective. Sometimes that helps shape the film in ways she can't predict. Another time I might have felt used. Instead, I felt part of some grand experiment that was maybe connecting Horace and Aida to a larger story taking place far away.

I dress quietly, but Mia wakes all the same. She turns her face, embarrassed at the sight of me bare-chested at the foot of her bed or, more likely, feeling naked without makeup. The Thursday morning caregiver will arrive soon. No time for us to talk about what did and didn't happen last night. This could be for the better.

Today's caregiver is about twenty years older than yesterday's. Margo is a sturdy looking woman with an air of the country girl in how she speaks. Her cheeks are puffy, as if she's been collecting food for the winter. I glance at Mia, expecting a look of disdain at Margo's corduroy pants and bulky sweater. Instead, they exchange warm smiles as she takes Margo's bag. She then takes Margo's arm, bringing her to the sunroom where Aida is clipping butterflies.

"You must be Aida!" Margo says. Her tone is pitch perfect, enthusiastic but not condescending. "I'm Margo. What beautiful butterflies! It must take a lot of patience to cut them out of the paper."

"Oh, I don't know about that."

But Aida reaches into her box for a few more clippings to show Margo.

Instinctively, Mia and I back off to the kitchen to watch the scene unfold.

"I hope you will not report this one," Mia whispers, her eyes teasing. "She has a good heart."

When Aida resists coming to the table for breakfast, Margo suggests a shower first to get cleaned up. To my surprise, Aida agrees.

"You don't need to wash her hair because we're taking her to the beauty salon later," I tell her.

Mia mocks the way I pronounce "salon." I'm strangely grateful. Her laughter brings my attention to the words, this expression hearkening from a time when we ate beef fondue, spread *Bain de Soleil* on our skin, and relaxed in the chaise lounge. For a moment I am transported back to this innocence.

After Margo's hour with Aida is up, I tell her we would like to see her more than one day a week. She blushes with pleasure, and tells us to contact the office. Maybe they can work it out.

After Mia sees Margo out, she finds me in the bedroom gathering clothes for a wash.

"So, when you call the office, are you going to denounce the girl who was texting?" she asks.

"Probably not. Like you said, I don't know her story."

Too equivocal. Her eyebrow raises, her head cocks to one side. She pushes me out of the way with the laundry hamper, which sends a few pairs of panties to the broadloom. Whatever I do—pick them up or leave them—will be the wrong move so I pretend not to notice.

Again, this insistence on protecting Texting Girl. Mia's sister blamed her for every mishap to avoid beatings. The French rounded up the Jews even before the Nazis had arrived in Paris. No matter what the scale, Mia hates anyone who denounces, snitches, tattles, and betrays. Never mind that reporting the caregiver's negligence is more like complaining to a company for not providing good service.

Mia only found out she was Jewish when she fled to her mother's house in France at the age of thirteen. Her mother had converted to Catholicism but felt obliged to tell her daughters the truth about their origins. The books on the shelf were so filled with hate against her people that Mia wanted no part of it, but it was already too late. Once you know something, she had reminded me, you can't unknow it. Unless you have dementia, I thought. Then you can unknow anything.

AT noon, Aida leaves the Meals on Wheels package on the counter again. This time I insist it's meant for her. Plying her with guilt that she is turning down a gift seems the only way to get through. Mia takes it one step further by taking a bite of her chicken pasta and scrunching her face into ecstasy as if this prefab meal is Cordon Bleu. I give her a reproachful look, as if to say, Stop treating Aida like a two-year old. Her glance says, Look who's talking.

Aida and I do the dishes while Mia packs her bag. I poke my head into her room, amazed at how many clothes she brought and how they all fit so well. For years, she'd said, even after she got her Canadian citizenship, she lived with a packed bag in the closet with her passport in the pocket. She doesn't trust authorities. At customs, especially since 9/11, they always pull her aside when they see she was born in Tunisia.

"I was never going to denounce the girl," I tell her.

Mia keeps her back turned, making like she doesn't hear me. Talking to her open suitcase, she says, "You trust me to get a nice haircut for Aida?"

"Of course."

"Because if not, I can stay here. I have emails."

"I wouldn't know what to tell the hairdresser."

"If you don't like what she does, you can always tell her boss."

"That's true."

I try to sound thoughtful and reasonable, knowing this will enrage her. I don't know where it comes from, this need to provoke. She bowls me over with the suitcase, ramming it into the side of my leg on her way out of the bedroom. In the space of a week we've become an old married couple.

I LEAVE Mia to manage Aida's haircut, feigning the need to run errands. I have no particular place to go or be. In a week, maybe less, they will discharge Horace, and he will expect to resume his old life. He has this display of war planes to build. Maybe that will be enough to hold him until spring. With the caregivers to help Aida with her pills and hygiene, and extra help coming from Veterans Affairs, I could leave them on their own again. This anxiousness in my gut, is it for them or me? If only a nice haircut would solve everything.

In their gated community in Florida, Horace and Aida were the most elegant of the inmates. Those who went for sports mostly took to golf, their sole exercise climbing in and out of the carts. Horace spent mornings on the tennis court playing doubles, which helped counteract the effect of the Christmas sweets. He touched up his hair as did Aida. All the other women were short, white-haired, and round, whereas Aida was tall, slender, and brunette. Genes, she would say, deferring the compliments. I wonder now if the blood condition was eating up nutrients and feeding the confusion in her mind. Or, if pecking away at food was a hunger strike to protest being left alone in the house so much. A silent cry for help from the silent Aida.

AIDA is admiring her new look in the mirror when I arrive to pick them up at the salon. Her hair is still white, but with the bob cut she easily looks twenty years' younger. The hairdresser, a woman in her early thirties with a face hollowed out from cigarettes, is glowing with pride. She'll probably give Mia the tip for pushing her out of her comfort zone.

By the time we're home, Aida has forgotten her new hairdo. She wants to know if we're going to see Horace, and I have to say No, not today, he needs to rest. And I grow sick at the thought of putting Mia on the train in a few hours, and coping on my own. With Aida back in her familiar chair with more decoupage cuttings, Mia and I silently agree to meet back on the hard couch in the living room to break through our morass. In an hour, the three of us will have an early dinner out and then drop Mia off at the station. If not now, then when?

We make small talk for a while. What she'll do in Montreal, who she'll see. She has no place of her own. She uses one friend's address for tax purposes and squats with another.

"I guess you don't like me so much," she says. "I'm too different. Too sick. I won't bother you any more with translation. You will have enough to do once your father gets home. But I hope you get some help. You can't give up your life for them."

I'm not fast enough to absorb all that Mia has unleashed.

"*Tu dis rien?* I've been here a week and you haven't kissed me. We slept in the same bed last night, finally, and you didn't touch me. I find this highly insulting."

A host of factors play into my reaction. Stress, fatigue, a horrible sense of missed opportunity and misread signals, a sense of impending loss, even anger that she is leaving. But what wins out is the idea that she is highly insulted from my apparent lack of interest. There is something both noble and ridiculous in this turn of phrase. I can't help but laugh.

Enraged anew, she pushes off the couch and disappears into the sunroom. A few minutes later, I see her bring Aida into the bedroom to get dressed for dinner. At loose ends, I haul her suitcase into the back of the Roadmaster. I would rather be packing up the flag stand for another run to the Cenotaph.

Dinner at the bistro is subdued. I spend it throwing out memories to Aida and then catching them myself. Mia refuses to look me in the eyes.

"Mia is heading back to Montreal after dinner," I announce.

"You are?" Aida says.

"Yes, I am planning for a trip to Tunisia. In North Africa."

"Africa!"

"We're going to miss her, aren't we, Aida?" I tell her.

"You'll manage," Mia says. "By tomorrow you won't even remember I was here."

"Don't worry," I say. "Aida won't soon forget you."

"Of course I won't."

"I'm not so sure about Ivan," Mia says. "He doesn't have a good memory."

"He's a good boy."

"Mia is going to research a new film," I tell Aida.

"Isn't that nice."

"She's got a boyfriend waiting for her," I add.

"A boyfriend!" Aida says.

It's Mia's turn to laugh.

"He's not a boyfriend, Aida. Just an old friend. I'm not sure where Ivan got this impression."

"Mia wrote all about him," I tell Aida. "He sounded like a boyfriend."

"He's an Arab. I'm like a sister to him. He would never touch me. Apart from the fact he's married and has a child. You would make a good Arab, Ivan. Or a good brother."

Lovers, friends, brothers, sisters, it all muddles in my mind. I reach across the table for her hand, and she pulls it away. Is she trembling from the Sickness or emotion?

MIA hugs Aida goodbye in the parking lot of the train station, and sits her back in the front seat of the Roadmaster. Then she sets off for the platform with me coming up from behind with her bags like some kind of manservant. It's not so cold tonight so we stand on the platform where I can keep an eye on Aida in the car.

Tears are welling up in Mia's eyes. She comes closer and I expect reconciliation. An opening, at least.

"Karim?" she says. "Are you crazy?"

Her finger stabs my chest in time with her accusations. Then she uses all ten fingers, fully loaded. She stares, waiting against all odds for a reasonable line of defence from me. The deafening announcement for an arriving train in both official languages gives me a few more seconds to think. And then another reprieve: the young woman with the burn mark on her face emerges from inside the station, wrapped in a flag of the Toronto Maple Leafs. She reassures us the next train is a freight. We shouldn't worry because it won't stop. The one after is for Montreal. It's been late all week, but tonight it's running on time.

"That's the girl I wrote you about. She's always here, whenever I come."

"I hate flags."

"It's for a hockey team."

"Even worse."

The roar of the freight train drowns out further talk for another minute. And then I tell her the truth:

"I'm sorry I didn't seduce you. I didn't want to mess up your film."

"My film?"

"Yes, by making things more complicated between you and Karim."

"You are the one inventing all these problems."

I turn slightly and catch sight of Aida getting out of the Roadmaster. I hold up my index finger to Mia and rush to the car before Aida gets too far. The roar of the Montreal train arriving drowns out my reassuring words to Aida.

"When are we seeing Horace?" she asks.

"Not until tomorrow."

"We can't we go now?"

"He's in Kingston, and it's a long way, and we'll get there too late for visiting hours. He's getting better, though, and he'll be home soon. Maybe next week."

"Next week!"

I don't know whether she's excited or disappointed.

"Can you wait for a few more minutes in the car? I'll be right back. I'm just saying goodbye to Mia."

"Mia?"

"I'll be right back."

Mia has moved down the platform, probably on the advice of Flag Girl. She is now perfectly positioned to get on the train quickly, especially since no one else is getting on and the conductor is primed to help with her bags.

"Mia!" I call out.

I stare into empty space, and then through the window of the train. I see her move down the aisle, but then lose her again. She must be sitting on the other side of the car. It doesn't matter because the lights in the train dim. I run up the platform to stand under a light with Flag Girl. Mia will see me if she looks my way.

WINTER 2010

29

HORACE HAS BEEN gone less than two weeks, but he's anxious all the way home from the hospital, convinced that he's missed a deadline for the *Reader's Digest* sweepstakes.

"They only give you so much time," he says.

"You're still in the running. I checked."

"They're looking for a reason to throw you out."

He unhitches his seatbelt as soon as the bungalow comes into view. While I help Aida out of the back, Horace is wobbling toward the garage door to find his flag. He wants it flying high before the outreach agent from Veterans Affairs shows up tomorrow. I quickly let Aida into the house, rush back to the garden to remove the pickle jar that is protecting the pipe in the garden from snow cover, and then meet Horace halfway across the lawn to help him plant the flag in the pipe. There are only a few inches of snow on the ground, but his balance is worse than ever. He's content to see the flag flying stiffly in the breeze, but once inside the house he flops limply into a chair in the sunroom.

"They don't want me to drive," he says.

"I know."

"If I'm sitting down, there's no problem. I feel fine."

Aida puts her arms around Horace and kisses him on the cheek.

"You're back!" she says.

I'm reassured she remembers that Horace has been away, but he squirms like a ten-year-old being smothered by an affectionate aunt. While Horace leafs through his mail to find the *Reader's Digest* envelope, I check my email. Nothing. Again and again, in English and French, I grovelled before the screen. Humour, sincerity, irony, anything for a sign of life, a kernel of forgiveness from Mia. A phone call was too risky for a control freak like me. She was a week in Montreal and has been in Paris for another three days. I like to think she had email problems here and can't get her French phone to charge. By the time it's sorted she'll be in Tunisia where the Internet connections may be spotty. I shouldn't give up all hope until after the 10th of December, when she's back in France. Which means about two weeks of uncertainty. I've had worse.

MARGO shows up just before eight o'clock, and seems to win over Horace by finding his favourite spoon in the utensil drawer. He sits at the table in his bathrobe reviewing the last missive from *Reader's Digest*. His mood sours as he watches Margo set out Aida's morning pills.

"I use an eggcup for those," he says.

"I thought we would try this coloured dish today. You can see the pills a whole lot better, don't you think? Because the pills are white and the dish is dark. And the egg cup is nice, but the pills are hidden down there because it's so deep, and Aida can't see them. What do you think, Horace, shall we try it this way today?"

He goes back to his cereal with a shrug.

"Look at your hair! You look so beautiful!" Margo says.

Aida shakes her head dismissively but is clearly pleased.

"We'll make sure we cover it up with a shower cap," Margo says.

After they disappear down the hall into the ensuite in the bedroom, Horace looks up at me. I'm standing in the middle of the sunroom, not sure where I should be or what I should be doing. I hardly slept last night from thinking about what Mia might be doing six hours ahead in Paris. It could be she's anxiously trying to get her email to see if I've written. How does she manage her pills with the time difference? She must find a way, with or without help. She thinks I didn't sleep with her because she's too sick. Maybe she's not sick enough. I take care of people too much, whether they want it or not.

"Who is she anyway?" Horace says.

"She's someone to help Aida with showers, provide a little company. Three mornings a week."

"Well, I'm back now. She doesn't need that."

"She wasn't getting washed properly before. And now you need time to recover from the stroke."

"I don't want her around."

"Why?"

"I don't need a reason. This is my goddamned house. I can take care of Aida. That eggcup was working fine."

He clears his throat when Margo comes back in the room. I give her a quick look and she moves to Plan B: asking about the flag. Her leading questions are pitch perfect. She clearly studied my notes, and easily gets Horace talking about the war. I tune out until the climax.

"We were at ten thousand feet, and the plane started doing this flip flop business," Horace says.

"That must have been terrifying, Horace."

"You bet your life. We were heading straight down. We could see the top of the trees. The plane righted itself in the nick of time. Two weeks later the war was over."

"You must have had an angel on your shoulder."

"That's right. The Creator intervened."

"And I'm sure he'll be looking after you and Aida now."

"That's right."

I give Margo a look that says, You were doing so well…

"The Creator and I can take care of Aida," Horace says. "You don't need to come in anymore."

I jump in with my own divine intervention.

"It might be nice for Aida to have a little female company. Why don't we give it another try? It's not every day. And the government pays for it."

I motion to Margo not to say anything.

"We could try one more time."

"Good idea," I say.

"Thank you, Horace," Margo says.

I motion Margo to pack up early while Horace is feeling positive about the visits. She hugs Aida and gives Horace a hug, too. Not scripted, but not a bad move. Horace makes an off-colour joke about being in his bathrobe, and Margo escapes without further injury.

The house descends into silence with Margo's departure. Even Horace seems to sense it. "Where's your friend?" he asks.

"She went back to Montreal. She's getting ready for her trip to Africa."

"They've got a hell of a lot of problems over there."

I'm not sure he means Montreal or Africa, but I don't engage him.

AROUND noon, Horace answers the doorbell, expecting Daphne McTavish—the outreach worker from Veterans Affairs. He starts on immediately about the war, pointing to the wall beside him, how he'll build his display of planes. The woman listens politely for a few minutes, hands him a paper bag, and turns to leave.

"You're not staying?" he says.

"I'm just dropping off the food for your wife."

"For my wife?"

Horace shuts the door behind her and thrusts the meal at me.

"They're a hell of an outfit," he says.

"It's called Meals on Wheels. They bring over a hot lunch three times a week.

"Cancel it. We've got our own frozen food."

He starts scratching his back.

After lunch, when the doorbell rings again and Horace doesn't move, I answer it. Daphne McTavish is on the short and round side, in her early thirties. Too young to be talking to old men about life after a stroke. Her hair is sensible, her eyes cautious not to give too much away. She has a pleasant smile, which reveals good teeth. That's a plus as Horace is a strong believer in proper dental care.

I sit quietly at the kitchen table while Daphne gets installed in the sunroom with Horace and Aida. She hauls a folder out of her bag, and hands Horace a flyer about the Veterans Independence Program.

"VIP, that's me," Horace says, grinning.

Daphne smiles like she's hearing that joke for the first time. She talks with the fevered pitch of an infomercial. A volunteer driver to help with groceries for several hours a week! Vouchers for frozen food! Housekeeping help! But wait, there's more! Someone to shovel the snow in winter and rake the leaves in autumn! And a walker to help you stay on your feet!

With no briefing from me, she nods and smiles her way through Horace's stories about the homemade flag, his friend Bob, and the miraculous recovery from the spin. A few minutes after she leaves, Horace's beaming face disappears.

"They've left me all alone," he says.

"She was just here, and they're offering you all this help. Someone to help with groceries. This is great!"

Yet he remains despondent, the silence in the room taken up with Aida's repetitive talk. If Mia were here, she would redirect Aida's attention, ply her hands with lotion, tell her funny stories.

Horace gets up abruptly.

"I'm going for the mail," he announces.

"It's snowed again. You want me to drive you?"

"Christ, it's just across the street."

He can't free the zipper in his ski jacket, which gets stuck halfway up. I wiggle it until it gets back on track, and he looks on gratefully. I watch him slip, slide, and waver down the driveway, concentrating so hard he doesn't look up at his flag. I want to follow him secretly.

He returns triumphantly with a package from the *Reader's Digest* sweepstakes, which looks like the music he ordered. There is something else. Two letters from the Ministry of Transport.

"I'll show you how to play these on the music box I got you," I tell him.

But Horace is not easily distracted from the ministry envelopes. He opens the one in his name, and hands it to me.

"What is this about?"

They've taken his licence away. Again. I did not have to denounce him to the government. Somehow the system did it for me.

"It's a reminder that you can't drive."

"Well, I knew that. I've got to get better."

I don't press the point. He tears open the next one addressed to Aida. Maybe the doctor decided to write the ministry about Aida's health. Two licence cancellations in one day. A miracle.

"Jesus, Aida is taking her test on the third of November. When is that?"

He hands me the letter. Yes, it's a reminder, not a cancellation. Just when you want the government to be inefficient. But it's on the thirtieth, not the third. Horace has been transposing numbers since he got back from the hospital. Common enough after a stroke, they told me. It should straighten itself out. For now, it presents an easy opportunity to park Aida's driving career where it belongs. Yet I can't face the look on Horace's face. Not the rage against the damned government I was expecting, but rather one of despair. Of not being able to keep up. Of a man whose miracles are running out. Then I'm swept up with my inability to let Horace experience anything negative if I can somehow save him, whatever the cost.

"It's not the third, it's the thirtieth. Next week."

"Well, then all our problems are solved."

"Which problems are those?"

"Not being able to drive."

"Winter is coming. You're not going to the cottage so you don't need a car except for errands. And the woman who was just here said you could have a volunteer driver for six hours a week."

My delivery is more breathless and intense than usual. I need to undo the hope I've just stupidly given him, or at least to make him recognize the good fortune. All these miracles he doesn't see.

"Six hours. What's that to me?"

"It's six hours."

"Aida can take this test. They want her to take it."

"Because they don't know about her memory problems, and that's my fault. I should have asked her doctor to tell them."

"You always want the government involved. Look what they did to me. Took away my licence for months, and I had to get it back. And now they don't want me to drive again."

Keep thinking that, please. In a week, once they're settled, I will take the car back with me to Ottawa for safekeeping. Again.

"Aida will take that test, and if she passes she should be driving. As simple as that."

"And if she fails, then it means she shouldn't be driving."

Horace considers this idea, and slowly nods his head.

"Only one way to find out."

"I can drive if you need to go somewhere," Aida says. "I can leave all this cutting out for later."

Horace doesn't answer Aida. He's too focused on flipping through papers and magazines on the end tables.

"Your *Reader's Digest* stuff is on the kitchen table," I tell him.

"No, I want the driver's handbook."

"It's at the cottage."

"With all the shutters on? Damn it."

"We can pick one up at the licence bureau or the library."

"Let's do that. First thing tomorrow."

It will break up the day, tracking down the driver's manual. As long as Horace doesn't get abusive about her inability to study, there's not much harm done—except for the potential humiliation of putting Aida through an experience she won't understand. If it can put the driving idea to rest once and for all, then maybe it will be worth it.

30

MIA IS PROBABLY sleeping now in the one-room apartment she shares with Bertrand, an old friend in Paris. I don't quite understand their arrangement except I know he's Tunisian. Jewish, though, so no proscriptions against sex. They are just old friends now. Sure they are. Bertrand was the one who brought them to Quebec in the late 1970s, after they had spent time on a kibbutz in Israel and worked on a farm in northern France. But he didn't like Montreal so he went home to Paris. Mia stayed. Somewhere before or after her two film degrees in Montreal, she met Karim who had arrived here after his time in Damascus. They maintained a platonic friendship centred around nostalgia. Then he gave up on Quebec as well, and went home to Sfax. Mia, the self-proclaimed nomad, seems a homebody by comparison.

I'm not clear if Bertrand stays in the apartment when Mia goes to France. I know he picks her up at the airport. I don't have the telephone number, either for the apartment or her French mobile. Why should I? It's not like we know each other. I spent a few weeks translating some texts for her film project. We wrote a lot of emails. She came to help out with Aida for a week. We didn't make love. And that's all there is to it, apparently, since she is not answering. Or maybe she's having trouble with her email.

Lying in bed, to put Mia out of my mind, I work out the rest of my stay here in Riverton. The key is to space all the caregiving visits over the week so they don't overwhelm Horace. I do this knowing full well that nothing works out as I've planned.

Yet this time, more or less, it does. In the morning we find the most recent edition of the driver's manual at the library. On Monday, I visit the drop-in program for people with Alzheimer's to see how Aida might fit in. On Tuesday, an occupational therapist fits Horace for a walker and recommends a railing for the stairs to the basement. On Wednesday morning, I interview three possible drivers, privately, at Starbucks, choosing the middle-aged Bible thumper who I'm sure will hit it off with Horace over his miraculous life. In the afternoon, the Lifeline people hook up an emergency intercom system activated by a bracelet on Horace's wrist. On Thursday morning, the city sends a housekeeper who seems to understand that visiting with Aida is more important than the cleaning and dusting. In the afternoon, the first box of frozen food arrives from Veterans Affairs.

All through the week, Horace encourages Aida to study the multiple-choice questions in the driver's handbook. He sits her at the kitchen table with a pencil, going over traffic signs. He snaps at her and, to my delight, she snaps back. I start work on the biodiversity text for Parks Canada at the dining room table. Apparently, park rangers regularly start forest fires to help regenerate ecosystems. A prescribed burn, they call it, as if everything is okay so long as the head guy gives you the go-ahead.

The Ministry of Transport holds the driver's test at the IGA in Prescott so Horace wants to pick up some food while he's waiting. He leaves his walker in the Roadmaster, preferring to grip the shopping cart. I stand outside the general-purpose room where Aida and about fifteen other seniors are sitting on plastic chairs behind four foldout tables. Some of them, like Aida, are struggling. Others are whipping through the questions and looking around the room for vindication.

"Are they still at it?" Horace asks, bumping into me with his cart. It's like old times at the Express Lane trying to beat the "one per family" rule. Except our roles are reversed: he's the one running into my heels.

As other seniors hand in their completed answers, Aida is still staring at the page. Horace marches into the room, sits beside her, and starts ticking off boxes. Love. Fraud. Self-interest. All of the above. He is simply removing an obstacle from his path, the way he would haul out a bent nail from a board with the claw of his hammer. No one notices. Sometimes a crime is best perpetrated openly. Mia would be pleased to know that I don't turn him in to the authorities. How could I when I reminded him to wear his seatbelt and fix his mirror for his road test? Besides, with Horace's dysphasia, I can't see him getting any more right answers than Aida. There is, of course, the possibility of more divine intervention for the Creator's Miracle Man.

I leave them huddled together under the overhang of the IGA while I get the Roadmaster. Snow is coming down fast. Horace waves me into the fire lane as if I don't see them. Aida waves, too. There's no denying we're family.

31

THE SCHEDULE I've set up for Horace is barely holding. He complains the driver doesn't jump when he calls her up for a grocery trip. Then there's Margo coming three mornings a week and the housekeeper on the other two days.

"The girl sits on her ass half the time and drinks tea with Aida."

"That's part of her job."

"You coming down this weekend? I want to get the board for my display. The girl's car is too small."

The girls are different people—the housekeeper and the driver—but I follow his thinking.

IT is strange to be home again, in the condo. So quiet except for these calls from Horace. Difficult to concentrate on the translation. I look outside at the snowy sidewalk, think of my tea with Karen, and wonder how she is doing in Montreal. I flip back to the text translated for Mia, and wonder how she is faring on her trip. Does she think of me? I picture Aida in her chair, cutting out butterflies, and Horace in the dining room table planning his display. The best part of my day is finishing the evening pill reminder and knowing that Aida will soon be safely in bed.

Apparently, even with a permit for controlled burns, a person is still liable if something goes wrong. We had a rusted oil barrel in the back forty where Horace burned things before the bylaws made it illegal. I remember standing beside the barrel as close as I could, seeing the flame through the holes, feeling the rush of intense heat. Nothing ever got out of control.

I get an email from Jerry, one of my hockey buddies. With his wife and kids visiting her parents, he's having a boys' night next weekend. I've been to his place once before. We sat around an official poker table in his man-cave with our beers in built-in holders surrounded by posters of dogs playing cards. Money and bad taste to burn. Yet I would go willingly, losing myself in one-upmanship stories of old conquests and new flirtations. I might even play along, embellishing my encounter with Mia to make it much more than it was.

In one of our post-game coffees last winter, I learned that Jerry and I played house-league hockey in the same west-end arena. He was a few years behind me, playing in Mosquito division when I was in Bantam. We went to the same high school as well, although he didn't play for the school team. He knew my friend Tom, which surprised me. I didn't ask if he remembered Karen from the band or mention that we had been married. Probably I was afraid of some revelation or else hoping he would speak of her on his own, and I would learn something new. With all these connections, real or imagined between us, our weekly beer league hockey games took on a special cachet. If Jerry didn't show up, the game held less interest for me.

When we were kids on early Saturday mornings in winter, before we started playing hockey ourselves, Tom and I would meet in the lobby of an apartment building on Baseline Road. This was before anyone thought to put locks on the front doors. Whoever arrived first warmed himself by the radiator. Then together we walked to the arena to watch the early morning games. I can't remember how old we were, but it was before Horace put me into extra French classes on Saturdays so I must have been eight or nine. We quickly got bored of watching. Most of the time we invented our own games, like kicking a scrunched-up pop can around. Sometimes there were extra nets stacked in a corner, and we took shots on each other with the can, much like we did after school in my driveway with a tennis ball, sticks, and goalie equipment. In one of the wire cages set up behind the goalies, Tom and I would flick the light switch when someone scored a goal. In real hockey games on television, a red light would come on. Here, the light fixtures were empty, but if we spit into the live socket it would sizzle. I had always thought water put out fires, but apparently it was not that simple.

⟶⊚ 32 ⊚⟵

WOULD MR. HORACE Pyefinch prefer to attend the Winner's Reception in his honour or receive his payout at home? They have helpfully enclosed a grid of Montreal to show the headquarters of *Reader's Digest*, as well as the nearby five-star hotel.

"You may wake up one morning soon to find that your life has changed... and that it will never be the same again," it says.

"It's so complicated," Horace says. "They send you all these stickers."

"They want you to read through everything so you buy something," I tell him. "Like that music you bought."

"I don't remember that."

I follow instructions to the letter, peeling, affixing, labelling.

"I don't care about the money," Horace says. "It would just be something to win. It would be another miracle to cap my life."

We drive lickety-split to the post office before looking for plywood. He's happiest here, I sometimes think. Standing at a counter with a captive audience who must listen to the stories of his wonderful life. When we enter Home Depot, with its cavernous aisles and busy clerks, his mood darkens. We're not planning to buy anything small, but I haul out a cart anyway so he can grip the handles. His new walker sits at home in the garage next to the oil drum and the flag stand. Maybe in the spring he'll get it out.

We find a helpful clerk in his late sixties who understands exactly what Horace wants. A miracle. Except the plywood is too big, even for the Roadmaster. Horace signs up for home delivery with a flourish. To hell with the expense, he says.

As usual Horace unhooks the seatbelt as soon as we're halfway down his street. His anxiety is contagious. I put Aida out of my mind when I'm focused on Horace's errands, but as soon as we come home a wave of fear sweeps over me. Somehow Aida has been fine alone up until now but will have a preventable accident in the time it takes for us to exit the car and enter the house. I'm not sure why Horace is anxious. Probably he wants to measure the wall where he will hang his display.

Aida is in the kitchen, pushing buttons on the keypad of the microwave until she finds the right one. Horace shakes his head, brings her finger up to the Start button.

"You see this piece of black tape?" he says. "I put it here so you'd remember."

In the old days, Aida might have said she didn't like his tone of voice. Today, if his tone bothers her she doesn't say. Instead she rolls her eyes at me. To mock herself or Horace, or maybe both together.

Her first microwave, a large and bulky affair, was a rare Christmas gift from Horace, hidden for weeks in the neighbour's garage and then unwrapped by Aida with singular pleasure. Early on, I had re-heated turkey leftovers wrapped in tinfoil, which set off fireworks inside, scorching the bottom.

I rubbed at the brown stain with baking soda, put another plate on top to hide the mark, as if they wouldn't know I was the guilty party.

HORACE insists that we get rid of all Aida's caregivers. He doesn't like these people coming and going. The woman who drives him around is good enough.

"Aida needs more stimulation," I tell him. "She can't sit around all day."

"She's fine."

"She couldn't even get to the day program last week."

"I don't remember that."

"You told me the driver came and she wasn't ready."

"To hell with all of that."

I don't argue with him about all the help for Aida, hoping he'll simply forget his objections. But on Sunday I sleep over rather than drive home to help Aida get ready for the volunteer who picks people up.

I pull slacks and skirts off the racks, holding them up with an encouraging look, fighting my impatience. We go through the entire closet twice before I understand she can't hold the idea of choosing an outfit in her mind long enough to decide. So I lay out an ensemble on the chair, much the way she once did for me and Horace. I want other people to like her. Even with my help we're running late, and I have to wave off the driver.

"I guess that's it, then," Horace says.

There is self-satisfaction in his resigned voice.

We've missed the ride, but I can still get her to the program at the hospital. Except Horace insists on coming along, even if part of the idea for all this is to offer the caregiver a break.

I know she won't do anything without him so I don't protest.

I watch unseen from an alcove, an overprotective parent spying on his kids' first day at school. They are the only couple. Aida gets swallowed up in the group, listening to Horace the way she always does. He speaks of how he signed up for the air force to avenge Bob's death and his recovery from the flip-flopping spin two weeks before the war ended. The idea of taking turns or sharing stories is foreign to him. He does not play well with others. Through our devotion to his every remark for countless decades, Aida and I created a Miracle Monster.

 33

Borrowed memories
12/13/2010 7:18 PM
From: mia hakim
To: Ivan Pyefinch

    I've always preferred the memories of others and expected to find them in Tunisia, not to bring them with me from Canada. Yet in my long silences with Karim in the car I think of this strange family I recently met, an old man obsessed with his own past, desperate to find meaning in it, to not forget, carrying his vanity and fear in equal measure, the weight of it pulling his shoulders forward. All this love of his own specialness, his flag, everything I hate, and yet something finally touching about it. The old woman, her memory almost gone, yet still sharp, seeing places the rest of us cannot. Her mind wrestles with the desire to forget, the need to remember. So eager to please and not bother, a silent woman all her life who is finding her voice and has no one to listen. And their son, because how else could I describe him? A man, yes, but a son first. So dedicated to his parents like a small boy who wants to please them, but not for gain or attention, only to keep them alive because once they are gone he will be lost, he who seems to love them more than he loves himself. He will only have words left, and they won't be enough. His heart, so tender, entrusted with their well-being, yet ready to denounce, yes denounce them for some higher purpose, and oh his heart cannot bear the responsibility. More than anything, yes, he would be free of the burden, but he does not see how, until they die. And his sweet words that you ignore, to punish him for hurting you, for putting them ahead of you, even if you have no rights, you, forever the outsider, the stranger, yes, that's what hurts the most, your inability to fit in, and there most of all, in an English town full of patriots and flags and traditions that do not belong to you. Your armour skintight so that even if he had touched you, you might have rejected him. You spoke of your Sickness to him, and you saw the fear in his eyes as you prepared your pills for the day, just the way he prepares pills for his mother. You cannot blame him, but you do. Because he can't see beyond the burden. Here with Karim, your heart rends at all the words unspoken with the son, the chances lost out of fear, your childish need to make him suffer as you have, and how you would give him the chance he so wants to prove himself. Not an impossible task you set, just something to show he can set you above all else, this man, who you think maybe you could, no, you won't say that word. So much to tell him about your journey, the selves you are discovering, the lies you've told to protect yourself.

 34

MIA'S EMAIL is more like a diary entry that she wanted me to find. I feel like I have become a character in her film. I am not in a lead role but rather a walk-on with no speaking part. Something cracks anyway, and a word slips out four times, almost involuntarily. It comes out in different registers—low, high, squeaky, whispered—as if I'm an adolescent whose adult voice is struggling to emerge.

Go, go, go, go.

An hour after I buy a ticket to Paris for Christmas Day, the caregiver calls. In the small hours of the morning, Aida's knee buckled as she got out of bed to pee. I can see her flipping back and forth, spinning out of control. The Creator did not intervene, and she landed hard, unable to right herself but determined not to make a fuss. At her insistence, Horace left her on the floor with a pillow and a blanket and went back to bed for an hour. Only then, with Aida immobile and wet on the carpet, did he call the woman who's been driving him around, and she called for help. It's like the *Reader's Digest* said: one morning he will wake, and his life will never be the same.

I sit beside Aida all day in the emergency ward while we wait for the diagnosis, and then all evening in the hallway while we wait for the surgeon. I hold her hand, reminding her she has broken her hip and wrist.

"I'd better smarten up," she says.

After the operation, I call Horace with an update.

"I've thought it all through," he says, interrupting. "It's so simple. I just need lag screws that come in through the wall in the garage. That'll hold 'er up."

When I reach the bungalow he demonstrates how he will mount his display of airplanes before he asks about Aida. I bring him to see her the next morning. She's in intensive care. Her blood pressure has dropped. They aren't taking chances.

He gets waylaid at the desk where a nurse asks if he had cut his nose.

"I wear these strips at night to breathe, and then I just keep them on all day. You want one? I've got an extra somewhere."

As he fishes through his pockets, the nurses laugh at this sweet old man.

I watch from the edge of Aida's room. He stays another

minute to demonstrate his device, leaning over the counter for his close-up.

She is awake, sitting up in bed with breakfast. He enters the room, centre stage, waving both arms like a rock star leaving after a third encore. I know you want more of me, they say, but this is all I can give.

—◦◦◎ 35 ◎◦◦—

Travels with Aida
12/13/2010 7:52 PM
From: mia hakim
To: Ivan Pyefinch

I never knew the silence of Aida, this coldness that enveloped her for so long. I do not understand its origins, can only guess at them. I only see how it is breaking now as her mind forgets, free at last to smile, laugh, cry, and lash out. We sat for hours, and I told her stories of my life that she would not remember. I found a travel journal in a drawer, her notes were sterile, and I wanted to infect them with feeling.

I think of her husband who takes up so much space, how it suffocates her, makes her swallow any words that want to emerge, how they spit out like bullets. No, like blanks, the kind of bullets that have no power. The hole in her heart a bottomless pit, all these emotions to be smothered before the wind catches them and they burn her up.

—◦◦◎ 36 ◎◦◦—

IT TAKES ME a few minutes to find the travel journal that Mia spoke about. As Horace sleeps alone in his bed, I sit in the sunroom in Aida's wicker chair to let her words pass into me unfiltered, and I let them steep before I stir them up with my own.

7 AM, Nov. 25/82

Crossed bridge 10:15 AM
Customs
Exit 22 Tylerville Road North
Knights Motel arrived 3:30 p.m.
Beautiful day little traffic.
Left Motel 7AM
Stopped at Xmas store.

THE new bulbs and thick garlands don't have the same allure as the ones in storage. Nor does she stay up all night to wrap presents and flood the living room with them. She longs for a special gift from Horace. That much hasn't changed.

They are so isolated in their rented condo by the ocean. In the seascape on the wall behind the sofa, a lone gull circles the dunes and grass under a cloudy sky. While Horace dozes in front of the television, she stares at the gull, trying to decide if it feels more real than the birds she sees over the ocean.

They visit friends at Beaver Dam Estates, a gated community peopled mostly by Canadians. There are country clubs, tennis courts and swimming pools, a golf course with real alligators in the artificial ponds, and courses to learn new crafts. Signs along the streets warn drivers to watch out for seniors having fun. She would not allow herself to hope. Only after they order a home in a new subdivision for the following autumn does dreaming seem possible again.

IT costs money even to visit the storage barn, but she insists. She wants to see her furniture up close again to decide what they will bring, what colours she would choose for the carpets and the walls. It seems most of her belongings are packed out of sight, but it doesn't really matter after all. She just wants to be near them again.

No matter how much she studies the blueprints, no matter how she measures and rearranges, she could not fit all her furniture and antiques from the two-story stone home into a two-bedroom prefabricated house. They would bring the living and dining room furniture, and the bedroom set. The gilded mirror, yes, that would go too, and the buffet and the armoire with the marble top. The rest she would leave behind, along with countless boxes. Perhaps it's just as well. She tries to believe that leaving the old creates space for the new.

She wraps the Royal Doulton figurine slowly with newspaper, first with the sports section, then with local news and last with the classifieds. The lady in fancy dress holding a purse needs plenty of reading material for the trip. With her body tilting slightly to the left, the lady has always appeared to be in motion. Her head, with the hair so delicately coiffed underneath her bonnet, also appears to be turning. You could think she is waiting for a friend to catch up or taking a last look at what she is leaving behind. A perfect going-away gift from Dot and other neighbours in Quebec all those many years ago. Remember us, it says.

She helps Horace set her precious antiques on dollies, and rolls them up the ramp of the rented truck. The weather has turned. They can see their breath. Her hands are cold because they have packed away all their warm clothes, including her gloves. She still can't relax, even after they are finally on the road, dragging the station wagon behind them and the heat blasting in the truck's cabin. Each bump on the highway, each blast of wind brings a chill to her heart. The mirror, even wrapped tightly in cardboard, could fall over. She does not want any bad luck to mar this latest dream home.

Nov 4, 1983 Friday

Left Riverton 9AM
Loaded with our furniture
for Beaver Dam Estates

AIDA and Dot clasp hands and marvel at the hands of fate that guided them both to this corner of Florida. They do not speak of how their correspondence faltered, of who was the last to write, of private sorrows. Instead, they enthuse about the retirement park and its amenities, of getting together with their husbands to catch up.

Aida, still thin and graceful at fifty-nine, her hair lovingly cared for to hide the grey, assesses her old friend's face to see what twenty-five years have wrought. In Dot's smile of recognition, Aida observes the crows' feet around the eyes, watches lines stretch out from her wide-open mouth.

She doesn't tell Horace about the encounter with her friend, not right away. Instead, in case Dot ever drops by unexpectedly, she dusts the figurine that sits on a shelf of the hutch in the dining room. The past is best experienced through wood and china.

IT'S her turn to host after their Thursday afternoon shuffleboard game. She bakes tray after tray of sweet nothings, confident they would impress her new women friends. They are white-haired, round, or mousy, and flirt with Horace. He sits between two women on the wicker loveseat, extending an arm around each one and pinching their ample waists until they squeal. Aida offers Horace another square, something to bring his hands back to her.

She had modelled once in a local fashion show to help raise money for charity. The clothes had been sensible and the audience mostly women. He had said nothing, and she'd heard him. She hadn't volunteered for the show again.

She would no longer wear a bathing suit, not for a fashion show, not for one of their beach parties. She would not even go near the pools. She wouldn't swim ever again. Yet she digs out her two-piece from the drawer for Horace, who wears it for a gag fashion show at the park. He sashays down the catwalk with his slender legs and tight stomach, putting a hand suggestively on his butt to the delight of the white-haired women. She watches with an enigmatic smile.

April 10, 1984

Left Punta Gorda 6:45 a.m.
Arrived 6 p.m. Days Inn
Florence – exit 157 – Rain
Price 28.88 disc. 21.14

THE Mona Lisa's smile was less appealing than her husband had imagined. She didn't mind. She had felt part of the girl's private memory. As he'd pulled her away to beat the crowd at the next big painting in the Louvre, she had taken one last look and her lips had parted slightly.

She has the same inner smile when they pull off the highway in Florence, North Carolina, as if she were one step closer to Italy. Paint peels off the ceiling and mould collects on the bathroom fixtures of their motel room. She lays towels on the bed and sleeps in her clothes, covering her eyes to protect against any flecks of paint that fall during the night. She imagines Michelangelo, lying on his back on a scaffold in the Sistine Chapel year after year to finish his masterpiece. Even if she is not a believer, it would be something to see. But with the house in Florida and the cottage along the St. Lawrence River, she dares not ask for more.

They stay at the same motel in a different room the next year. She holds her breath before opening the door. The walls have a fresh coat of paint. She still sleeps in her clothes, imagining frescoes of unspeakable beauty on the ceiling above.

Punta Gorda – April 17/95

We
Had a nice room & were
lucky Antique Car Show on
Everything booked.

THE car rally was foretold, if only she had checked the back pages of her travel journal for Carlisle in April. She should have known not to linger at Carolina Pottery. They might have beaten the rush.

She stares out the passenger-side window into the night, wondering if Joseph blamed Mary for slowing them down on the way to Bethlehem. He dragged her from inn to inn, determined to provide for his wife and the unborn child, ignoring her stumbles along the cobblestones. He has not told Mary everything the angel said.

Horace finds them a room, a nice one. It's a miracle.

Horace

had a long chat with someone
from Chatam for the car show

SHE carefully removes the tissue that protected her purchase: a handmade vase decorated with daisies in relief, so real looking she could have almost plucked the petals off. He loves me. He loves me not.

She wonders if Mary saved the wrapping paper from the gifts of the three wise men or if she tossed it past the sheep and goats into the bale of hay behind the manger. Did Mary resent they brought her nothing? The excitement of birthing a saviour fades after a few minutes, and Mary is left alone with a bawling infant. She can hear Joseph and one of the wise men outside the stable talking about the crowds, how fortunate they were to find a place.

Back inside, he recaps the conversation she has already heard through the thin walls. Normally, she would interject to show interest but not tonight. He takes her silence for rapt attention. She is not sure how to spell Chatham. Was it "hem," like Bethlehem and the edge of a dress? So strange: cars and Carlisle, chats and Chatham. Maybe it is all meant to be.

April 25/97

Surprised to meet Bob & Barb Harrison
we had a drink in our room
& decided to have dinner across
from the motel

SHE does not look her best, not after a day on the road. She worries her slacks are too wrinkled, her blouse too ordinary, her ears too big. Maybe the liqueur will cloud their friends' judgment, at least about her ears.

They are like couples in old movies, enjoying pre-dinner cocktails in the drawing room except they have been standing beside two doublebeds drinking out of plastic cups.

She has to write their names in full, even after knowing them for seven years. They are winter friends, easily confused with other white-haired couples.

> *Left 6 had breakfast in Wilk Barre*
> *With Harrisons exit # mix-up*
> *Stopped & declared customs*

SURELY they would uncover her secrets, the way sometimes she wanted the spring floods in the park to rise up past the back step, sweep into the kitchen, and drown her; how five years ago the doctor had told her about the blood problem and given her ten years to live; those new moments where she mixed up numbers and names. Horace's word is good enough for the border guard. As he waves them through, she smiles at her deception.

> *Punta Gorda April 9, 99*
>
> *Horace had cramps in*
> *His right leg.*
> *Bought a tire traffic terrible*
> *Two lanes traffic for over*
> *Two hours*

SHE doesn't mind not driving. She much prefers the roles of

navigator, record-keeper, sounding board, masseuse. She likes time for her own thoughts to percolate, especially now when they are so often jumbled. She is never sure if she's already said something. Better not to say it at all, she decides.

Their neighbour at the cottage recorded the names of ships, and the dates and times they had gone up and down the river. He dies so young, just after retirement. She wonders what has become of his travel book.

THE last two trips to Florida and back go unrecorded, Aida's mind already wandering too far afield to tame her thoughts. Maybe after they leave the sunshine for good and buy the new bungalow in Riverton, she keeps heading south. In Carlisle, she will buy a vintage Jaguar and the wind whipping through the open window will bring back gusts of warm memories.

I send this reverie to Mia. A gift, an invitation, an apology. All of the above. Then I forward my itinerary for a flight to Paris on Christmas Day because even my spontaneous acts are planned.

37

I WANT AIDA to stay in the hospital, away from the casual indifference of Horace, so she can get better. But patients do not tarry here. It is a way station. He counts the days until her return, when he expects everything will go back to the new normal. He cannot imagine she will not come back, how his son has used his power of attorney to jumpstart the process for a nursing home, then evaded the questions of the hospital discharge team, made them think this was a family decision.

Aida is not safe at home. Leaving her on the floor while he goes back to bed—these are not the actions of someone who can be trusted. And there are the mysterious bruises on her wrists. So why do I feel like a traitor to the cause?

It could take weeks, maybe months, before a room opens in one of our three nursing home choices—choices Horace agreed to in such cavalier fashion never imagining that age and infirmity could afflict the Miracle Man. Yet a room becomes available for Aida in days. With luck, I can still make the trip to Paris, although it will be hard to leave Horace alone over Christmas.

HORACE sits at her bedside in the hospital, holding her hand. It's the kind of tableau that ruptures my confidence that I know best. For once Aida is not nattering and Horace is not talking miracles. Maybe, at some level, they understand this is a turning point.

The nursing home director arrives, beaming with the confidence of a clergyman. I have briefed him on what to say and what to withhold, but he goes off message. Horace seizes on the promise that Aida will be settled within two weeks.

I don't explain there is no coming home, even if she's not settled.

We detour to the cottage to retrieve the table saw for a new project—finishing shelves along the wall of the garage at the bungalow. He wants more space for orange juice and baby food containers for nails, washers, and lag screws.

"So you're going to wrap up your project by Tuesday," I say.

"I've got no timetable."

"If Aida were to come back to the house, you couldn't work on your projects."

"What are you talking about?"

"She needs round the clock care."

"I could always tie her to a chair if I go out."

There it is, the crystallization of my fears. Yet still I don't press the attack. I file it away for future reference, to be retrieved at an opportune moment.

THE telephone ring jars me awake. At this hour, it must be Horace. I could let it go to voicemail, but it sounds insistent.

He wants Aida home. Now that her hip is on the mend, he can take care of her. He will push their bed against the wall and sleep on the outside to protect her from falling.

"It's not your decision," I tell him.

"Don't tell me what to do."

"I'll be coming in a few hours. We'll talk about it some more."

"Don't bother coming."

I swing the receiver against my bookcase, chipping off some wood but leaving the electronics unscathed. My bedroom telephone is a sturdy Northern Telecom model. It was built to last.

--◉ 38 ◉--

An image of love
12/15/2010 3:26 PM
From: mia hakim
To: Ivan Pyefinch

It is his first heartbreak, this death, and he will never open his heart so big again. Horace holds onto his suffering, it feeds him, he would be lost without the memory of his friend. It's not the bricks in the box that make it so heavy, it is the photo.

—◉ 39 ◉—

AIDA SITS IN a wheelchair, a loaner from the hospital, dressed in her winter coat and boots that I have brought from home as we wait for the ambulance to show up. We're a low priority and there's no telling when it will arrive. They have orders to come to her room so we can't even wait in the lobby where we could watch people come and go. It would give me something to talk about. For two hours I've been telling her that we're going home knowing she won't remember. It's a nursing home so I suppose it's true. Pinetree Manor. The other two nursing homes are Lodges. They sound so stately.

When the ambulance shows up, we arrive at the Manor at shift change, the worst possible time. I can't tell who's coming and who's going. At least the halls are decked.

Aida gets another loaner wheelchair and we're left sitting in a corner until they're ready for us. The director of the Manor appears from the office, beaming again. He addresses her by name, which impresses me. Yet I can't help but think of my old high school principal who started every morning with a joke over the PA system. They both seem too eager to please. Worse, he's trying to please me, not her.

Most of the nurses and support workers are white women, which makes the South Asian woman and the two male nurses stand out. Manny, one of the men, takes charge of showing

Aida to her new room. He gets her laughing within seconds and I allow myself to think everything will be fine here. Except her room is in the old wing, which faces south but still manages to be dark and overlooks the parking lot rather than a garden. Her roommate is a woman in a wheelchair who seems semi-conscious. Getting Aida settled—unpacking a suitcase, putting some knickknacks on the shelves—takes some time, but not as much as I need. After it's over, what will she do? I stretch out my movements as long as I can, deflecting her questions about why she's here and the whereabouts of Horace. At three-thirty, we've missed the afternoon bingo game and dinner is about two hours' away.

Manny returns with a support worker to get Aida into the bathroom. I can hear them explaining how to pull the cord by the toilet to let them know she's done. After, I tell them Aida won't remember.

"In that case you can push this button on the bed when she's ready," she says.

I don't ask what happens if I'm not here. I feel like I've entered a prison where the rules are clear only to the longest-serving inmates and the guards. Should I palm the nurse a chocolate bar to make sure Aida gets good treatment?

After she's lying in bed, I do the paperwork and then set off to explore the inner workings of the Manor.

"Ivan!"

It's Margo, the caregiver. I'm so delighted to see a familiar face I almost utter "You? Here?" as Horace might do. She works at the Manor most afternoons, helping animate some of the more sedentary residents. She brings them to the social events at two o'clock or to the alcove with the fireplace. Could she find time for Aida? Yes, she could.

"She's in line for a single room," I say. "I don't know how

long that might take."

"I'll keep an eye out for you on that, Ivan."

Underneath Margo's country girl exterior lurks a woman who knows how things work.

"The Christmas dinner tomorrow is sold out, but I bought a few extra tickets," she says.

"I'm flying out tomorrow night to see Mia in Paris."

"That's so nice! But the dinner is early so maybe you can still make it."

If there's judgment in her eyes or voice, I don't hear it. Her dimpled smile radiates nothing but good vibes. I'm the one who feels like I'm abandoning both Aida and Horace. The least I can do is squeeze in some turkey before I go.

Aida's room is so dark that I blink to adjust to the difference. She welcomes the affectionate embrace from Margo. All those years of thinking Aida was shut down only to find it takes so little to open her up.

"They haven't put the alarm on, Aida!" Margo says. "Let me fix that up for you. We wouldn't want you falling out of bed!"

"No, we wouldn't want that!"

Yet falling out of bed is exactly how she got here. What I always considered to be the safest place for Aida turned out to be the most dangerous. Horace might not have acted right away, but eventually he did call for help. Would the staff here be so quick? The halls are like the Star Trek Enterprise on red alert. Somewhere the lights must be sounding on a switchboard. I don't see people walking on the double. I don't even see them walking on the single.

"I have to go, Aida," I tell her. "I'll see you tomorrow."

And with a kiss on one cheek—the English way—I flee the room, the comatose roommate, the dreary walls of the old wing, the vacant nursing station with the switchboard ablaze with calls for assistance. I guess right on the corridor to the front door, punch in the code to let myself out, and then drive off without trying to figure out which window belongs to Aida's room.

—— 40 ——

The revolution will be televised
12/20/2010 8:23 AM
From: mia hakim
To: Ivan Pyefinch

A young street vendor set himself on fire in front of the police prefecture in Tunis. He is still alive, but his despair and desperation have lit a fire under the feet of Ben Ali, the dictator. Unemployed people, high school students, teachers, journalists, they are all protesting. I have come back to Paris too soon. I am the Queen of Bad Timing.

—— 41 ——

ON THE REFRIGERATOR door in the bungalow, Horace has stuck a January 2011 calendar and circled the fourth of the month. Beyond the date when Aida's supposed to have "settled" into the nursing home, I'm not sure what it represents. I like to think it will mark his acceptance of this new life passage. More likely he will declare that she is "unsettled" and insist she come home. This would explain why he has no interest in the Manor. Of course, it's full of old people, which depresses him. But since he believes Aida will be coming home in a week there's really no point in visiting. He prefers to concentrate on a new project at the dining room table, something involving poster tubes, red paint, white Letraset, and green plastic apples. Although I've said that I'm flying out to Paris tonight, I'm not sure it has registered. I don't disturb him with words, simply squeeze his shoulder in farewell.

I CAN HEAR support workers in Aida's bathroom so I wait for her in the visitor's chair. On the other side of the room, the husband of her roommate is preparing to feed his wife. Her mouth opens automatically at the pressure of a spoon against her lips. Such devotion. Horace can't even manage to eat in the dining room with Aida. How would he cope if Aida deteriorated further?

A curly-haired support worker, maybe twenty-three, emerges from the bathroom. As she heads over to Aida's dresser, she doesn't see me sitting in the gloom. I scrape the legs of the chair to get her attention, making her nearly drop the pair of underwear in her hands.

"Your mother had an accident," the young woman says.

She says the words so casually it takes a few seconds for me to panic.

"She fell?"

"Oh, nothing like that. She wet herself. It's just… you may need diapers."

"It's never happened before. She just needs someone to help her out of the chair."

"We do what we can."

Her shoulders lift slightly as she speaks the words. Not a shrug exactly. More a gesture of resignation designed to lower my expectations. Diapers would make it easier for everyone.

The dining room has been lovingly appointed with Christmas cheer. Snowflakes cut from construction paper by local school children are taped on the windows. Each table has a small poinsettia and a tea candle. A brightly decorated tree stands in the corner, and traditional arrangements of carols waft through the PA system. She soaks up all this atmosphere with a beatific smile, grasping the hands of one tablemate in greeting and stretching over to help another with her bib. Alone in her room Aida seems withdrawn and lost, but here, surrounded by so many people who need help, she finds purpose. I allow myself to believe she will be better off in the Manor than cutting out paper butterflies in her sunroom at home. No doubt the turkey wasn't basted all day and the stuffing is probably from a box, but it certainly beats the frozen food Horace has been feeding her for months. She cleans her plate, another sign that if the food is good she will actually eat more.

After dinner, I wheel her into the fireplace room where the fake coals and a music box with Christmas favourites allow us to keep the warmth of the season alive a little longer. In a half hour, I need to be on the road to make my flight. How to do so gracefully is the question. A few others are joining us near the fire with their family members. Maybe I can escape.

"So what's next?" she asks.

"I thought we would sit for a little while and enjoy the fire."

"Where is Horace?"

"He was really tired tonight."

"When am I going home?"

"We've got to get your hip fixed."

"Oh, that's right. Where is Horace?

"He's at home making you a present."

But this white lie only aggravates her because she has nothing to give him. So I lie again, reassure her that we had bought him a sweater together a few weeks ago. A young girl arrives delighted by the fire and the Christmas tree in the corner. Aida compliments her dress, and I seize this moment to slip out of my chair. I stand off to one side for a few minutes. Aida keeps talking to different people. She doesn't notice I've gone.

AGAIN, that mix of giddiness and guilt at passing through the locked doors of the Manor. If I set out now for the airport at a good clip, I'll have maybe forty-five minutes to spare. Except I can't find my passport. I check my shoulder bag three times, and then my hand luggage. Inexplicably, I must have left it at the house. Which means another awkward farewell, if Horace even remembers that I've gone.

The front door is unlocked so I slip into the house unnoticed. At the end of the hall and around the corner I can hear the television blazing. With luck I can find the passport in my bedroom and be out the door again with Horace none the wiser. It all goes according to plan except that I glance into the dining room where the chandelier is still lit. On the table I see what looks like a child's craft project—newspapers spread atop the massive plywood that sits on the dining room table, scissors and Scotch tape, a tube of dry cement, a paint brush soaking in a pickle jar, and his four tubes, painted red, standing like sentinels. I move closer and see four vertical rows of white letters in Letraset arranged on the table. I imagine he will tape the letters vertically on each tube, but I can't make any sense of it until I realize that, put together, the four tubes spell horizontal words.

A I D A

W I T H

L O V E

E V E R

"Once the paint dries, I'll glue on the letters," Horace says. "I think it will make a nice gift for Aida."

It would be so much easier if Horace were monstrous all the time. These moments of kindness and affection and—yes, let me say it—his love for Aida, disarm me. I can't make him take a taxi alone to the nursing home tomorrow.

He turns off the living room light and watches me walk to the front door.

"Where are you going?" he asks.

"To get my bag from the car."

⚭ 42 ⚭

Monster
12/24/2010 6:25 AM
From: mia hakim
To: Ivan Pyefinch

So I woke up today, excited you're coming and I read your mail that Aida has broken her hip and is now in a wheeling chair, and that all this happened weeks ago. Everything I have written and sent you seems false because you were not really present, how could you have been? You must think I am some kind of monster that you could not tell me this before now. But I don't understand if Aida is safe, why you can't come and leave Horace on his own for a week. You cannot baby them forever, you need to let them grow up...

—◦◦ 43 ◦◦—

HORACE IS GLUING letters onto the red tubes before he has poured his cereal or found his favourite spoon. He finishes the last tube, and puts it with the others.

A I D A
H I T W
E O V L
R V E E

"Oh, no," he says. "It's all wrong. All that work."

"It's fine, really. If you switch the first and the last tube, it will read perfectly. It's because there are two "As".

"It says 'Aida', but nothing else makes sense."

Horace stares uncomprehending at the letters, convinced of his grievous mistake. I watch his lips move silently as if he wants to force the words to have meaning. Is it another stroke? Here is my chance to play the hero, to make it all better, and start the morning with him in my debt. But I want him to figure out what's wrong. The man who built a cottage from scratch must surely be capable of figuring out this puzzle. Yet he grows more despondent.

I reach out to adjust the tubes and he pushes my arm away.

"It's in the wrong order," he says. "There's nothing else the matter with it."

Rather than elated or relieved, he sounds disgusted, as if the world has conspired to set it up wrong. On the lid of each poster tube he starts to dry cement a green, plastic apple. I'm not sure what the apples represent, but the red and green are Christmas colours so maybe that's enough meaning. No sense in projecting more onto Horace than is really there.

"Did you want me to get you a bag for the tubes?" I ask.

"They're not going anywhere. She'll be home inside of a week."

"So this is not a Christmas present?"

"The head guy said she'd be settled in two weeks. I don't think she likes it there. Who would?"

He's made the tubes as a homecoming present. For this, I gave up Paris. For this, I disappointed Mia.

"It's Christmas today, and it might be nice if you gave her this as a present for her room."

Horace contemplates this idea, and nods vigorously.

"I just need to find a large bag," he says.

BLOWING snow makes the drive treacherous. We slip and slide along the highway until we reach the Manor. The parking lot is almost empty. Our visit lasts just long enough for Horace to put the tubes on her shelf. There is nothing to do, not on Christmas. No physio today, no Margo, only the basic routines. Nothing to say except that he wants her home. Surely he could fix Aida's hip with some duct tape, shake loose her memories with a few squirts of WD-40.

We leave her in tears.

"I could bring her home at least for lunch," Horace says.

"Not a good idea, especially with the wheelchair. She won't understand why she can't stay."

"And why can't she stay? I can look after her."

"Like tying her up in a chair, you mean."

"I don't know what you're talking about."

"She has to stay in the nursing home."

"It's not your decision. The head guy said two weeks."

"She's not coming home again. You'll have to get used to the idea."

My words of truth come unbidden from a mysterious part of my brain and out my mouth before I really know what I've said.

"The hell with that and the hell with you, too. You can leave now. I didn't ask you to be here. And you can leave the car."

While Horace storms around the house, I call the police. On Christmas Day, they are surly, impatient with this query about the legalities of me holding onto Horace's car. They are not interested in what might happen if I leave it. They certainly don't have the resources to keep an eye out for the Roadmaster and a man driving without a licence. And if I keep the car against his will, Horace could charge me with theft. The cop transmits this message with a certain satisfaction in his voice. Mia is right. I need to let them grow up and grow up myself. Unto this day is a saviour is born, but it's no longer me. The son of the Creator's Miracle Man is closing up shop, putting himself out of business, letting the parents fall where they may. I leave the keys to the Roadmaster on the antique buffet that sits across from the wall that will feature his display of war planes. I could hide them, but that doesn't seem to be playing fair. If this weather keeps up he won't be tempted. Without a goodbye, I take a taxi to the train station where not even Maple Leaf Girl is out on such a blustery day. It pleases me to think she has a family, and may be opening presents or perhaps helping her mother with Christmas dinner. The fierce wind covers up the echo of my furtive cries to Mia on the platform. I hope she is spending the evening with friends in my absence, although since she's Jewish I'm not sure what, if anything, this day means to her.

—◦◉◦ 44 ◦◉◦—

Belonging
12/28/2010 7:18 PM
From: mia hakim
To: Ivan Pyefinch

    I was lonely through Christmas and Hannukah, and maybe that is why I went to the protests. All the Tunisians in Paris, Jews and Muslims, we marched to the embassy shouting slogans. I was crying all the time, for those who are fighting the real battle back home, for all the years of oppression, for my lonely childhood, for this feeling that I belonged somewhere, at last. My hand was shaking, the way it does, but so was everyone else's.

—◦◉◦ 45 ◦◉◦—

"THEY'VE GOT A hell of a set-up," Horace says over my speaker phone. "They've got her walking between two rails, and they watch her. They really know what they're doing. I could never do that back home. One more week now and she'll be using a walker."

I stay silent on the telephone, certain one wrong word will set him off.

"How is your display of planes coming along?"

"I've got another project going in the basement. I'm stringing a clothesline to hang up some of the old clothes. I found my old bomber jacket. It's brittle as hell. Do you think you can take it to a dry cleaner? Maybe they can do

something with it. Aida will be so surprised when she sees all
her old dresses up there."

─◦◉◞ 46 ◟◉◦─

Changes no one believes
12/30/2010 4:05 PM
From: mia hakim
To: Ivan Pyefinch

    The lawyers in Tunisia are joining the protest in solidarity
with the people. The president has denounced all this as
politically motivated. Ben Ali is making cosmetic changes in his
cabinet, but no one takes it seriously.

─◦◉◞ 47 ◟◉◦─

"I'M CUTTING them off," Horace says, over the phone. "I
want her out of there. I can take care of her."
    "It's not your decision."
    "It's my money. It's my wife. What the hell are you talking
about? Who's going to stop me?"

─◦◉◞ 48 ◟◉◦─

Tunisia is burning
1/5/2011 9:18 PM
From: mia hakim
To: Ivan Pyefinch

    Mohamed Bouazizi died from the burns. The students
are not returning to classes, and the lawyers are organizing a
strike. In some cities, protestors are storming public buildings

and setting them on fire. Police are shooting into the crowd and more than fifty members of the big union have been killed. They have called in the army now.

 49

"THIS IS DUNCAN Pook from the Manor. Your father showed up in a taxi today when Aida was in the middle of her physiotherapy session. We asked him to sit for a few minutes, but he wouldn't listen. He took her out of the physio room and was running down the hall pushing her in the wheelchair. The staff tried to stop him. When he couldn't manage the security code to open the front door, he rammed Aida in her wheelchair against one nurse, he took a swing at Manny, and slapped a female nurse in the face. We had to call the police. The nurses may press charges. I'm sending him a No Trespassing order for 24 hours. Does he have access to firearms? Please call as soon as you get this message."

 50

More lies
1/12/2011 9:46 AM
From: mia hakim
To: Ivan Pyefinch

Ben Ali has given a speech where he says the protestors are terrorists. He has promised to create 300,000 jobs and hold a conference on employment next month. No one believes his lies. The people wave the national flag in the streets. For the first time in my life I find this moving and not offensive.

―❦ 51 ❦―

"I WANT YOU to arrange another location for Aida. They are prohibiting me to go to her room. I'm going to see my lawyer. They don't know who the hell they've got on their hands now."

―❦ 52 ❦―

Curfew
1/13/2011 6:58 PM
From: mia hakim
To: Ivan Pyefinch

Tunis is raging, in the heart of the city and the suburbs. Many people have been wounded by the army, and the government has imposed a curfew. The big union is finally calling for a general strike. I am so frightened that I sit by my computer and wait for emails from Karim. He says there is hope in the air.

―❦ 53 ❦―

"I'M GOING to attempt to visit Aida. I'll be waiting for the police and ask them to bind my two hands so I can't protest and hurt them. I'm going to stand at the Cenotaph with my uniform and my flag until they let her go, and I'll be wearing it to see the lawyer. I've called the newspaper, and told them what's going on here. They know me there."

⟨⟨ 54 ⟩⟩

Desperate for power
1/14/2011 10:27 AM
From: mia hakim
To: Ivan Pyefinch

Ben Ali now promises to end repression and censorship. He will lower prices on essential goods, and not run for re-election in 2014. But he also replaced the head of the army who refused to shoot civilians.

⟨⟨ 55 ⟩⟩

"IT'S DUNCAN Pook again. Your father ignored the No Trespassing order. He showed up with a police escort. He went straight into Aida's room, and took away the four tubes on her shelf. He said it was his property. Aida was in the dining room so she didn't see any of this. I'm discussing the situation with the Board tonight."

⟨⟨ 56 ⟩⟩

Horra, horra
1/14/2011 11:08 AM
From: mia hakim
To: Ivan Pyefinch

"Ben Ali, alla barra, Tounes, Tounes, horra, horra!"
"Ben Ali dégage, Tunisie, Tunisie, libre, libre!"
"Ben Ali, get out, Tunisia, Tunisia, freedom, freedom!"

—◦◦◉⟩ 57 ⟨◉◦◦—

"IT'S DAVE COUSINS from the city desk at *The Recorder and Times* in Brockville. I wanted to let you know your father called us to say he plans to stand at the Cenotaph with a gun until your mother is released from the Manor. We all know Horace, and we're very fond of him. We talked a lot about this at the office, and decided to call the police. He seems pretty wound up."

—◦◦◉⟩ 58 ⟨◉◦◦—

The courage of an old man
1/14/2011 11:18 AM
From: mia hakim
To: Ivan Pyefinch

There was an old man on the streets in a rage, defying the police. The crowd was just behind him. They were ready to explode if the police touched one hair on his head.

—◦◦◉⟩ 59 ⟨◉◦◦—

"THIS IS DR. GOLIGER. I received your message about Horace. Unfortunately, my hands are tied. The law says I have to see a patient within seven days before recommending any kind of mental examination. If he comes in to see me, then I can make an initial assessment."

-⦿ 60 ⦿-

Afraid
1/15/2011 7:04 AM
From: mia hakim
To: Ivan Pyefinch

A massive march against the government, and Ben Ali has run away to Saudi Arabia. The people have won and now I'm frightened about what happens next. I need to digest everything.

-⦿ 61 ⦿-

HORACE COULDN'T manage the box full of bricks so he must have been planning to stand with the flag or march with it, as if he were on strike. He was clever to stay on the river side of the highway, off the Manor's property so he wouldn't violate the restraining order. It should have been safe on that side, right on the shoulder of the road. But he stowed the lighter fluid behind the driver's seat, and had to stand on the edge of the highway to open the door. Maybe he took a few steps back to allow the door to swing open and shut again. Then maybe he got too far ahead of himself. He started thinking about lighting the flag, and how long he could stand with it burning. Would cars honk in solidarity? How long before they released Aida? Would he make headlines around the world like that Tunisian fruit vendor who set himself alight? All those thoughts. Maybe the sight of Horace in his air force uniform, with the flag leaning up against the tailgate, distracted the driver in the other car. All this may be too grandiose. The reason for the accident may be much simpler. When I picked up the Roadmaster from the highway, I found the picture of Horace and Bob near the front tire. He must have removed it from the flag stand in the garage. Maybe he was planning to hold it up for all to see with his free hand, or secure it to the flag somehow. He might have dropped it, then chased it into the path of the oncoming car.

SPRING 2011

THE FUNERAL in the church where Horace and Aida got married is overflowing. When I speak my eulogy, I glance at Aida in the front row beside Margo. I hesitated to bring her here. What purpose would it serve? Certainly not "closure." She smiles up at me, not registering that my lament is directed for Horace. Margaret from up the road at the cottage also speaks. She tells the story Horace loved to tell, how he once held her in the palm of his hands.

I move into the bungalow for as long as it takes to sort through papers and junk, make sense of the finances, and ready it for sale. Starting in the garage so I can create some space, I find boxes and trunks with draperies from the living room of my childhood home, swatches of material for dresses never made, clothes that are too small, too worn, or too outdated. If I keep looking, surely I will discover some deep meaning to why they moved this junk around with them for fifty years. Childhood toys, my grandfather's wooden wheelbarrow broken into its constituent parts. I am drawn to the humidifier, the one-time watering hole for my western action figures. Johnny West and Captain Maddox would scan the area for dead rattlesnakes before allowing their horses to drink or filling up their own canteens. No need today. The reservoir is dry, long abandoned. My throat is parched as I toss it into the dumpster on the driveway. I visit Aida every day, gradually accepting that the nurses can manage her medication better than I can. I think of Mia and her butterfly box, and the alarm on her phone for her pills.

I have little time for translation so I fob it off on Karen, who is only too happy for the work. She is surprisingly compassionate about my loss, considering how little she cared for Horace. She even offers to help me clean up their house, but this would involve her staying over, which feels too complicated. My head is still spinning from playing musical bedrooms with Mia.

Mia has stopped writing, maybe because I stopped first. She doesn't know about Horace. She wanted me to stop babying him, and now I blame her for my poor decision to leave him the Roadmaster. In rare flashes, I see this as my own kind of immaturity, a refusal to accept responsibility. Even rarer are those moments when I see my remorse as yet one more example of grandiosity, this belief that I know best and can control all outcomes. Most of the time it's easier to blame Mia because the pain of not knowing what was going through Horace's mind on the highway, and if I could have prevented the accident, is too much to bear. At last word she was planning a second trip to Tunisia because the revolution has changed the focus of her film. Her own story now will be situated in something bigger—the role of women in bringing down the dictator. Some evenings I follow the constitutional talks in Tunisia on the French websites, and wonder if I will hear from her again. Other nights I take all my recorded voicemails from Horace and edit them into one long pastiche. For what purpose I'm not sure, except to hear his voice imposing his happiness, reflecting on his good fortune, even berating me, is much better than enduring the silence in the house.

In this way two months pass.

In April, the real estate agent sets up three candles to rid the empty basement of its musty smell. With all the newspapers and magazines recycled, and the financial papers shredded, there is nothing left to catch fire. Still, I check on the candles a few times a day, ostensibly to find peace from the auctioneers hauling away the furniture and valuables that I'm not keeping. But it feels sometimes like entering a sanctuary and before I blow out the candles in the evening I stand before them, one at a time, and close my eyes. I would not have believed simple candles could perform this cleansing, but the agent knows her stuff. Take everything out, she says. Clean and paint it. Pretend it's a new house. I know that even a personal photo on the refrigerator can throw off a potential buyer. Yet I insist Horace's flag must fly in the garden. If it weren't sewn up against the frame, I would fly it at half mast.

With the painters ready to start, I throw out the last mattress and slip into the car for one last spin before the Car Heaven people pick it up. The Roadmaster Buick Estate is now an end-of-life vehicle. Once they drain the harmful chemicals, they will scrap it. There are lots of worthy causes that could receive the proceeds, but I choose one that encourages kids to study math and engineering. I like the idea of leaving the car to science.

When I turn over the Roadmaster, it coughs and protests. I floor the gas pedal, until I hear the voice of Horace in my head: *Stop! You'll flood the engine!* I ease up and give the engine fifteen minutes of calm before trying again. In the meantime, I check the glove compartment, knowing I've already emptied it. I flip back the sun visors in search of errant receipts. I tuck my fingers into the crack between the seat and the back cushion, and touch some coins. I can't manipulate my fingers in the small space to retrieve them. The best I can do is push them along and hope they emerge. Instead they fall into a deeper crevice out of reach.

—◦◉ 63 ◉◦—

AT FIRST, the sound waves appear as an indistinguishable downpour of vertical lines on my screen, but then I zoom out, creating individual islands strung across a vast river. Their shapes are identical above and below the horizontal line, but the small ones seem farther away, as if in perspective. Stretched even more, those implacable islands blur and break up into jagged peaks, rolling waves, signposts, and then, nothing at all. Horace's voice crests and sinks.

AIDA wants to talk to you, but you're not there, it's just a recording. *Bonjour mon vieux. Je suis ici maintenant pour cet après-midi.* I would love to learn French. How about you teaching me? Thought we'd say hello and tell you what kind of a horrible day weather-wise it is. It's blowing like crazy. A terrible storm. White caps all over the place and raining like hell. Hi, it's me. Horace. I went down and picked up a cap identical to mine. The only difference is that it's two dollars instead of five. I don't know whether you have an affinity for hats, or not hats. We've got a whole bunch of those special muffins that we love so much. They were on sale. When I got to this Enterprise organization that rents cars, I ended up with confusion. I couldn't make myself understood. I was speaking, but there was no sense to what I was saying. So anyway, they drove me home. I went to bed and had a sleep, and when I woke up, I was quite normal. I thought I'd give you a buzz. Aida and I just had a real nice listen to Paul Anka's history. There's nothing happening. Hello? I'm missing it here. I'm writing this to my doctor in desperation. You can see the mark on my forehead from smashing my fist there from my frustration. The itch continues unabated. There doesn't seem to be any way to find out why I'm sick. I can't continue this desperate way. It's just unbelievable that this is happening to me. Can you find a way to bring me back to normal? I thought I'd give you a call. I get lonesome for you. It's Horace. I didn't know if you were still alive. I'd like you to give me a call. I want to see how loud the phone rings because we might miss it. So now the head guy has cut my ability to visit my wife. I can't believe you're all ganging up on me. It's awful. When you get this call me back if you're ready to do anything. *Bonjour, c'est Horace ici.* Just back from downtown with a huge bag of used bananas, ripe bananas or whatever. Ninety-nine cents. Christ, I'm going to look like a banana. It's Horace, of course. There's something screwy in the television again. We get four channels, but we can't increase the volume or anything. I was just wondering if you had any ideas what's caused this. Anyway. Whatever. You can forget that last call.

64

I MEET KAREN in the Bridgehead below my building rather than buzz her up to my condo. The weather is too cool to sit outside, although they have tables set up on the sidewalk in the hope of a sunny day. Her clothes are less forcibly chic this time round, but she still busses me—Montreal-style—on both cheeks. It feels tender rather than perfunctory, which I presume has to do with me losing Horace.

I give her the cushioned seat, while I take the industrial stool. The magnanimous gesture is automatic, and I regret it instantly.

"Guess what?" she says. "I'm moving back to Ottawa."

She delivers the news with searching eyes, as if she expects a welcome home gift. I am, to my own surprise, indifferent to where she lives. Yet how easily I fall into the old habit of giving people attention when they crave it.

"With Luc?"

She shakes her head dismissively.

"He was too young for me. Not enough life experience."

Another smile, shyer this time. As if to say, "Not like you." Taking care of elderly parents to excess is apparently no longer a fault.

"I need a place to stay until I get settled. I was wondering, since you're not using it, if you'd mind me staying here."

Her head motions upwards, presumably toward my condo on the fifth floor rather than the heavens. Now that I'm back it's not possible, but I have a perverse need to string her along. Maybe because I suspect her kindness and compassion over the last two months have been leading up to this moment.

"When did you decide to move back?"

"I don't know. What does it matter?"

A flash of the old Karen before her smile takes over. Defiance and hurt mixed together, making me think there's more to the story of her and Luc. I don't press. I'm not really interested in knowing that either.

"You could have, but I moved back this week."

She looks crushed, near tears even.

"I can lend you some money if you want, for first and last month's rent."

"How much have you 'lent' me already? And you've fed

me work for months."

"We're still friends."

"You take such good care of me."

"That's why you left."

She laughs because it's true. I smothered her with paternal kindness, the same way I smothered my parents, the same way I smothered my chances with Mia. Yet it would not take much for me and Karen to try again. I'm sure Luc has dumped her, and she's rebounding. An invitation to spend a few days on the couch, which would turn out to be a week in my bed. She's vulnerable and needy, as am I because of Horace's sudden death, worrying about Aida, and yes, missing Mia.

They are similar, Mia and Karen, in one way. This penchant for arriving unannounced. I plan everything so carefully. No rough edges, no chance for the unexpected. Always the dutiful choice.

"I've changed my mind," I tell her. "You can stay in the condo."

She looks up, confused, surprised, pleased.

"I'll stay out of your hair," she says. "I won't even shut your drawers."

"You can stay here on your own. I'm taking a holiday."

"Just like that? That's not like you. Where will you go?"

"*Tunisie.*"

The French word emerges from some deep place of longing, unplanned. One less syllable than the English, as if I have no time to lose.

Acknowledgements

I am grateful to Valerie Compton and Isabel Huggan for advice and feedback; to Wendy MacIntyre for unflagging support and encouragement; and to Emery Moreira at *8th House Publishing* for bringing the novel into the light.

I would also like to thank the Canada Council for the Arts for the grant to write this book; the editors of *Mitra* magazine for publishing an excerpt in 2018; and the jury of the *2020 Guernica Prize* for selecting the novel as a finalist.

Finally, I am indebted to the late Michka Saäl for her edits on early drafts. Her notes for an unfinished film called *Souvenirs empruntés* inspired Mia's journey and, ultimately, the form of the novel. *Borrowed Memories* is for her.

ABOUT THE AUTHOR

MARK FOSS is the author of the novels *Molly O* and *Spoilers*, as well as the short story collection *Kissing the Damned*. His fiction and creative non-fiction have also appeared in *The Fiddlehead, The New Quarterly, subTerrain, Numéro Cinq, carte blanche, Montréal Serai* and elsewhere. A radio drama, *Higher Ground*, was broadcast on CBC. He lives in Montreal.